JESUS CHAN AND THE RETURN OF MAYAN MAGIC

MARCOS ANTONIO HERNANDEZ

CHAPTER ONE

"THANK YOU, Dr. Martinez, for that wonderful introduction," the young man said in English as he took the stage. His well-fitting light gray suit looked custom-made, with the slightest break at his black wing tips, and the product in his black hair—parted at the side—shone in the glare from the studio lights overhead.

He started pacing across the stage, the red TEDx logo behind him, nodding his head as if gathering his thoughts.

"It's been three years since we've determined, conclusively, that the Maya Codex housed at the National Museum of Anthropology here in Mexico City is, in fact, the fourth existing example of Mayan writing that survived the Spanish Conquest," he said without a hint of nerves. He turned to the monitor and pointed the remote in his hand at the massive screen hanging behind him, bringing up a scan of a torn light brown page. In the center were two human figures drawn in the Mayan style, one standing while holding a rope that wrapped around the kneeling second figure's neck. Mayan script surrounded the figures.

"And what have we learned since then? Behind me is the god of death—"

"Man, Hugh talks so much better than you," Rodrigo said to Jesus, in Spanish, pulling both friends' attention away from the video they watched on Rodrigo's phone.

Jesus reached forward, turned off his friend's phone, and caught a glimpse of his own reflection in the dark screen. While his twin didn't have a single hair out of place, his own messy hair covered part of his high forehead with slight curls. Jesus stood a little straighter, hoping he could capture for himself the way Hunahpu—who went by Hugh—seemed in complete possession of himself and the way he presented to those around him.

Rodrigo pocketed his phone. "He put the video on his Facebook page," he said.

"I'll watch it later," Jesus said before he turned his attention to a pair of tourists arriving at the Great Museum of the Mayan World in Merida, far from Hugh in Mexico City. It was clear the two visitors were American from the way they dressed, and this was confirmed once they withdrew a large wad of cash and separated the Mexican pesos from the dollar bills. Jesus accepted their payment and waved them through.

"When's the last time Hugh came back to the Yucatán?" Rodrigo asked once the visitors sauntered away, speaking to each other in excited English.

"Christmas for a few days. Bugged us about moving to Mexico City with him, said we could live better over there," Jesus said, shaking his head.

"I'm assuming Señora Chan said no?"

"Of course! My mom will never leave. Too close to la energia, she says."

"My dad says the same thing. The older Maya got something in their head about this place," Rodrigo said, looking outside at the city beyond the museum's glass walls.

Jesus followed his gaze and wondered what his mother saw, or felt, within the Yucatán that kept her tied to the land of their ancestors. Maybe if he knew, he could explain for himself why he never left.

The sound of dress shoes clacking on the tile floor pulled Jesus's attention back into the museum. Approaching him from behind was Santiago García, the patrón of the museum, pointing out various exhibits to an older white man wearing a navy blue suit. The four members of Santiago's security team, whom Jesus called his pistoleros, followed two steps behind the pair, dressed in all black. Jesus had no idea how the García family made the money that funded the museum, but there was no denying that whenever the eldest son visited, he was a god passing through his domain. Always stylish, he wore a cream-colored linen shirt tucked into maroon pants and a tan fedora, his black belt matching his black dress shoes and the single stripe on his hat.

Jesus shoved his friend away from the front desk and further into the museum. The push made Rodrigo drop his phone, which fell with a loud clatter that reverberated throughout the open space and drew the patrón's attention.

Rodrigo picked up his phone and inspected it. "You're lucky it didn't break," he hissed.

"Everything all right over here?" Santiago asked as he walked over.

"Yes, sir, Señor García, just helping this guy get into the museum." Jesus looked at Rodrigo with wide eyes and tilted his head.

"Santi, just Santi," the patrón said, laying a hand on Jesus's shoulder. It wasn't the first time he had insisted on the nickname. "You made sure he paid, right?"

"Of course," Jesus lied.

Santi stared at Jesus as if he knew the truth, that Jesus let Rodrigo in for free a few times a week so his friend could offer tours for a few pesos without working for the museum. In fact, Jesus was sure Rodrigo would search for the Americans and use the opportunity for English practice.

"Are you the one running the front desk?" Santi asked with a slight tilt of his head while inspecting Jesus from head to toe. It wasn't the first time they had met, but Santi's eyes held no sign of recognition.

A wave of self-consciousness washed over Jesus, and he became aware of his darker skin and how he was the shortest person among the group.

"What's your name?" Santi asked.

"Jesus."

Santi waited for a moment before asking for his last name.

"Chan," Jesus said before pushing his lips together, knowing the name's Mayan roots. It was the most popular last name in the Yucatán state, an area known for a majority of its population being Mayan speakers.

"Ah, makes sense. You talk like your family's from around here," Santi said, turning away.

Although Santi didn't say it outright, Jesus knew what the man meant when he mentioned his family—that he was indigenous, a Maya, and therefore a step below in the social hierarchy. Santi didn't see Jesus flexing his jaw after encountering the familiar stigma once more.

Santi looked around the immediate area, searching. His group stood by, the pistoleros unmoving and the older white man watching the patrón in fascination. He found a tall, baby-faced young man a shade lighter than Jesus emptying a trash can nearby, just graduated from high school and brand new at the museum—so new, in fact, that Jesus forgot his name, having only heard it once.

"You," Santi said, approaching the young man, who looked terrified at the prospect of approaching the pistoleros. "Set that down, I need you to work the front desk." He put his arm around the scared employee and walked him back towards where Jesus stood. "Cheer up! You're going to be the first face people see when they get here!" he said, tapping the young man on the chest with an open hand.

Jesus's boss, Isabella, appeared around a corner farther behind Santi and the promoted employee. "Santi, I didn't know you were paying us a visit today," she said, her tone cordial but lacking warmth. A sliver of hair had escaped her messy bun and fell down the left side of her face.

"Showing one of my business partners our heritage," Santi replied with a smile, pointing to the white man in the suit but not making an introduction. On the surface, he was proud of the ancient Maya that ruled over the Yucatán before the Spanish Conquest, but that goodwill ran out when dealing with any of their descendants. "Now, son, you just stand here and make sure the visitors pay," Santi said, positioning the new employee behind the front desk.

The young man stood frozen, unsure of what to do, having received his previous orders from Isabella and now caught up in Santi's whirlwind energy.

Isabella dropped her chin and looked at Santi over her glasses. "Jesus is taking care of that," she said, raising her eyebrows.

"Not anymore." Santi turned to Jesus with a hard stare.

Jesus waited for Santi's accusation, the coming diatribe about how letting people in for free amounted to stealing from the museum and, in turn, him.

"There was a spot on the floor back there," Santi said,

pointing back in the direction he first came from. "Grab a mop and clean it up. You're in charge of keeping the place presentable!" the patrón said, flashing a smile.

Isabella met Jesus's gaze and apologized with her eyes. Being mestizo—a mix between Spanish and Maya—she had a foot in both doors, belonging to neither. And she understood what had happened without anyone telling her outright.

Jesus walked away from the front desk as Santi asked Isabella if she would like to join his group on their walk around the museum—a veiled command for a personal tour with the woman in charge of curation. Knowing she had no choice in the matter, she replied, "Gladly," and Jesus could hear the hidden strain behind her cheerful response despite not seeing her face.

After retrieving the mop bucket from the janitor's closet, Jesus walked back along the path of Santi's approach, looking for the spot the patrón had mentioned. It didn't exist. Instead, he mopped imagined spots so it looked like he was working hard for when Santi and his group returned. He continued on through the museum, passing Rodrigo talking in broken English to the American tourists, who followed behind and tolerated him but didn't engage. Over time, he caught up to Santi's group and mopped the floor in front of the displays opposite their position.

Santi's guest must've known Spanish, because Isabella's tour was spoken in the language even though she was fluent in English. They paused in front of an example of Mayan writing. "Here we can see the Mayan script. The Maya believed that the written word has the power to survive the death of its author, that it preserves human existence. I'd say most people take writing for granted." Isabella paused, waiting for the tentative nod from Santi's guest. The pistoleros stood behind in a shroud of seriousness as if her words weren't meant for them. One of them, a severe-looking woman with short jet-black hair, turned her attention to Jesus when she noticed him eaves-dropping.

He started mopping again right away.

Jesus had heard Isabella say similar things at the exhibit whenever she gave tours to other distinguished guests. He always enjoyed imagining a reanimated spirit springing forth from the page and standing alongside whoever read it, nodding in agreement.

Isabella continued. "The Maya didn't take writing for granted at all. They believed words surviving the author's death was a miracle!"

"How old is this?" Santi's guest asked.

"This is just a replica. The original, I think, is something like eight hundred years old?" Santi said, looking to Isabella for confirmation.

"Roughly," Isabella said, nodding.

"You said this is a replica. Where's the real book?"

"Well, they're not called books—they're codices, because they're made from bark instead of traditional paper. Most of them were burned by a Franciscan friar in 1562. This particular example comes from the Dresden Codex, in Dresden, Germany, one of only four that survived."

"Mexico lent them overseas?"

"Not quite—" Isabella began.

"They were stolen," interjected Santi.

"One is still in Mexico. The other three are in Europe—Dresden, Madrid, and Paris."

"Why don't they give them back?"

"I wish it were that simple," said Isabella.

Santi looked at the replica and a dreamlike spell washed over his face. "One day, they'll be back here, in Mexico."

An awkward silence descended on the group. "Why don't we keep moving?" Isabella suggested.

"I think I've had enough of museums," Santi's guest said. "This is all very impressive, and I think I'm ready to sit down and talk numbers about the new art space in Merida."

"Of course, of course," Santi said, putting a hand around the man's shoulder and turning around. He looked at Jesus and the drying spots extending down the hall.

"Great job!" he said. "Looks fantastic. Your talents shouldn't be wasted on something like the front desk." He turned to Isabella. "Keep an eye on this one, he's good!" Then, he started walking away with his guest, his pistoleros following behind them, leaving Isabella and Jesus alone.

Isabella walked towards Jesus as he put the mop back into the bucket with more force than he intended.

"Sorry about that," Isabella said, a twinge of sadness in her eye.

"It's all right," Jesus replied.

"Go back to the front desk. I'll see what I can do about giving you a different job so this doesn't happen again, but for now, stop letting your friends in without paying."

CHAPTER TWO

AFTER WORK, Jesus hopped on the bus that took him down Calle 60 towards the center of the colonial city. He got off before the busiest streets of El Centro and made his way to Parque de Santa Ana, where his mother owned a fruit stand that specialized in a variety of smoothies featuring chaya, also known as tree spinach.

She had his agua de chaya con piña waiting for him when he arrived.

"How was work?" she asked while picking through a bushel of chaya leaves, breaking off and throwing any brown bits on the ground.

"Same as every other day," Jesus lied while putting his backpack on one of the chairs behind the counter.

"No Americans gave you any trouble because of your English?" Beatriz asked, knowing her son's chief concern with his new responsibility.

"No," Jesus said, chuckling. "What words I know are good enough for what I do."

All of a sudden, the workers from other restaurants in their grove of food stands started barking out how they had tables available, and the best food. Looking towards the center of the park, Jesus saw a young man and woman walking hand in hand, making a beeline for the establishments. Ignoring the individual restauranteurs, the pair chose a table with a white tablecloth, and the associated vendor hurried towards them with two laminated menus in hand. The men responsible for the yellow, red, and green tablecloths returned to their conversations and current guests, another rejection taken in stride.

"Abilio, why didn't you say anything?" Beatriz said to Jesus's cousin, who had stood idle while the pair approached. Without taking his foot from the planter ledge surrounding the tree in front of her stand, he turned his head, shrugged, and told her he could tell they didn't want fruit.

"They were here for a meal," he said, flicking his dangling cross earring with his left hand before inspecting his nails. "I know what I'm doing."

Beatriz shook her head. "You know, sometimes you're more trouble than you're worth!"

"Love you too, Auntie," Abilio replied, blowing her a kiss with his darkened lips.

"He's going to be the death of me," Beatriz said to Jesus with mock seriousness.

As the sun went down on the day, Beatriz, her son, and her nephew took care of the tourists and locals who came by for all things fruit, charging the tourists a bit more. At the end of the night, they rolled the metal door down and started the walk home through the streets of Merida bathed in night.

Their home was on the other side of the train tracks to the east, beneath red-and-white metal towers connecting power lines that hung overhead. Beatriz unlocked the metal door in the concrete wall and held the door open for her two boys so she could be the one who made sure the door was locked after they all got home. Abilio took a bag of chips he'd bought sometime in the days before from the counter, plugged in his headphones, and lay on the couch while scrolling on his phone. Jesus sat at the table near his mother while she prepared their typical dinner—chicken, rice, and beans.

"Have you heard from Hunahpu lately?" Beatriz asked while putting a pot of water to boil.

Jesus smiled inside when he thought about how frustrated his twin would get if he heard his mother call him by his proper name, which he shared with one of the legendary Mayan hero twins, instead of his chosen shortened version. "No, not since he was here for Christmas. But Rodrigo showed me a video of his talk, he looked good."

"A talk? About what? He never tells me anything!"

"Something about the Mayan writing he's studying at the National Museum of Anthropology."

"Pull it up and show me!"

Jesus took out his phone, navigated to Facebook, and found the video Rodrigo had showed him earlier, the most recent post Hugh had made. While she cooked, Beatriz alternated between listening and watching her son talk about the different compounds found on the codex, from the thin layer of minerals that coated the bark paper to what constituted the various pigments. Jesus did his best to translate the English presentation, and despite not knowing a lot of the technical terms, he passed along the gist of the talk to his mother, who beamed with pride.

"When's the last time you talked to him?" Jesus asked once the video finished.

"Earlier today. He called to tell me that there's an open space near his house that would be perfect for a little shop," Beatriz said while stirring the beans.

"What did you tell him?" Jesus said, putting his cell phone

back into his pocket.

"I told him that sounded nice, that someone might be able to start a little fruit stand there." A mischievous glint sparkled in her eye.

"And what did he say to that?"

"That it could be me!" she said, laughing.

"He won't give it up," Jesus said, crossing his arms and putting both elbows on the table.

"He's wasting his breath. I told him now that you have a new promotion, we don't have anything to worry about!"

"About that . . ." Jesus began, trailing off.

Beatriz picked her head up from seasoning the chicken and looked at her son, waiting.

"Isabella didn't say anything about more money, just the new job."

"Well, it's on the way. And we'll figure something out until it gets here—we always do."

Beatriz made a plate of food and set it down on the table before informing Abilio that dinner was ready. When her nephew didn't respond, she marched over to the couch and ripped his headphones from his ears. "Come eat," she growled.

She made another plate and set it down in front of Jesus. Other than during that brief period after Hugh left their home and before Abilio arrived, he was always served second.

Beatriz scooped a smaller serving of rice onto her plate and looked at Abilio, who had a forkful of chicken and beans halfway up to his mouth. "Wait; don't be rude. How many times do I have to tell you?"

"Making sure you still have your wits about you, Auntie," Abilio said with a grin.

Beatriz shook her head; the crinkles around her eyes gave

away the smile she couldn't hide. She finished making her plate and sat down at the table. Then, she folded her hands and bowed her head, saying grace. Jesus had his hands folded while waiting for the prayer's end, his eyes still open, and when he met his cousin's gaze, Abilio rolled his eyes while still holding the fork in his hand, the other end resting in his food.

"Amen," Beatriz said at the conclusion of her prayer, lifting her head.

"Amen," her boys said in unison before digging into their food.

The young men took two bites for every one of Beatriz's, but since she gave them twice the food, they all got through their meal at the same rate. She paused between bites and sighed.

"Flaco died today," Beatriz said with sadness.

Jesus paused eating, while Abilio showed no sign of slowing down and responding. "What happened?" he asked.

"They said it was his heart."

"He was old," Abilio said with a mouthful of food. After catching Beatriz's glare and knowing he had gone too far, he added, "But it's never easy. How's Gloria handling it?"

"Tough, as can be expected. They were married for over forty years. I'm going to go sit with her tonight during the vigil."

"When's the mass?" Jesus asked.

"Haven't heard yet, but probably Wednesday. I'll leave Abilio in charge of the stand while I go."

Abilio nodded while taking another scoop of food with his fork. The rest of the conversations attempted during their meal couldn't pierce through the shroud of death that enveloped the room.

Jesus told Beatriz that he would take care of cleaning up. "Just go get ready," he said. "And try and be back in time to get some sleep."

"You don't need much sleep when you're old," Beatriz said as she walked into her room. Minutes later, she reemerged wearing the black dress she reserved for funerals. At her age, she used it far more than she liked.

"I'll have to plan the trip to Chichen Itza alone this year," Beatriz said behind Jesus, who had his back turned while washing dishes. She stood in front of her herb plants that lived on the windowsill, humming a tune while inspecting their new leaves and growing stalks.

Jesus rested his soap-covered hands on the edge of the sink. "Can't believe it's already the spring equinox again," he said.

"Sneaks up every year," Beatriz said. She added small sips of water to her herbs. "Gloria won't want to miss the return of Kukulcán, but she's in no condition to plan."

The ancient Maya believed that Kukulcán, the feathered serpent god, symbolized all life on Earth. The snake lived below and above the Earth and, with wings, could rule over the sky as well. The three planes of existence.

"How can you go to church multiple times every week and still believe in the Mayan god?" Abilio wondered aloud.

"We all have to believe in something," Jesus said, opening his eyes wide and setting his jaw as a warning to his cousin. "Besides, don't act like you aren't impressed with how they built the main pyramid in the perfect position for the shadow from the steps to align with the stone serpent head on the ground during the equinoxes. It really does look like a snake."

Beatriz grabbed her bag, slung it over her shoulder, and turned to her nephew. "Look, I might as well cover all of my bases, right? Keeps me safe. That's why I have Hunahpu, from the Mayan myth, and Jesus," she said while walking over to where Abilio sat on the couch. She leaned over and planted a kiss on his cheek.

Abilio was smiling when she pulled away.

"Don't wait up," Beatriz said as she walked out the door.

As soon as she left, Abilio sprang up and ran into the room he shared with Jesus, returning with a metal box Jesus knew he kept under their bed. While Jesus dried the washed dishes, Abilio withdrew a tarot deck.

"Want to pull a card?" Abilio asked, holding up the deck and shaking it at his cousin.

"Why are you bothering her about believing in God and Kukulcán when you believe in tarot and Santeria?" Jesus asked, shaking his head.

"I'm not saying she shouldn't believe in something. But the only reason we don't all believe in the Mayan gods anymore is because the Catholic Church came and ruined it for us!"

Jesus finished drying the dishes and started putting them away. "Don't let other people hear you talk like that. Religion is all that some of these people have."

"Whatever, I'm used to being an outsider—and I wouldn't have it any other way. Looking this fabulous all the time isn't easy, you know," Abilio said while pursing his lips and fluttering his eyelashes.

Jesus stared at his cousin until they both burst out laughing. He finished putting the dishes away then plopped down on the couch and pulled out his phone. Abilio, sitting cross-legged on the floor, had a series of cards arranged in a pattern in front of him.

"What are the cards telling you about our future?" Jesus asked.

"This isn't about our future. I'm trying to find out if the man I met is going to be the one." Abilio paused, deep in concentration, before flipping over the next card. "Interesting . . ."

"And?"

"There's a good chance he prefers women." Abilio gathered the cards to him and arranged them into a single pile. "We'll see about that," he said with a confident slyness. Then, he fanned the deck and held it up to Jesus. "Just pick one."

Jesus rolled his eyes and shrugged. "Fine." Reaching out, he hovered his hand over the pile, waiting for a sign or feeling telling him which card represented him. Not detecting any cosmic energy whatsoever, he exhaled, feeling foolish for even searching in the first place. Then, he pulled a card from the middle and held it up, showing Abilio without looking at it himself.

"Well, looks like you're in for an adventure, cousin!"

Jesus turned the card around and saw a zero in the center of the top edge, above a man on the edge of a cliff with a sack on a stick slung over his shoulder and a small dog at his feet. "What's it mean?"

"It's the fool. And, since it's upright, it means you're starting a new journey!" Abilio took the card and put it back in the deck. "Just don't forget about your poor old cousin, ok?" he added.

"Of course," Jesus said, before returning to his phone.

"Well, I think this is as good a time as any for a spell," Abilio said, wiggling his fingers in Jesus's direction and raising his dark eyebrows. "I've been saving this one for just the right time."

"You and your magic," Jesus said, not turning away from the screen in front of him.

"You won't be saying that when we get more money." Then, he pulled out four bundles of green herbs, five yellow roses, honey, and a small vial of something called esencia de dinero from his metal box. He boiled the herbs and roses in a few gallons of water while Jesus ignored him, filling the house with the smell of patchouli, then walked the mixture into the bathroom.

The sound of splashing reached Jesus, and his curiosity forced him from the couch. Upon entering the bathroom, he saw the steam from the mixture rising above the tub before Abilio waved him from the room.

A few minutes later, his cousin emerged back into the main room and told Jesus, "It's time. Go into the bathroom."

From what Jesus knew about Santeria, he expected to see a shrine of candles in front of a statuette of a Catholic saint, maybe an offering in a small bowl. Or worse, blood, if his cousin was dabbling in the most potent form of magic. Instead, he saw a single yellow candle burning on the bathtub's ledge.

"That's for the goddess of money. That's her favorite color," Abilio explained when he saw Jesus inspecting the candle. "Let me add these now that it's cooled down," Abilio said, shoving his way past Jesus. The honey and the esencia went into the tub, followed by a single index finger stirring the mixture in long, slow strokes.

"Ok, now get in."

"No way," Jesus said, backing up.

Abilio wouldn't take no for an answer. "You first, before your grand adventure, then me."

Jesus knew his cousin wouldn't give up, so he stripped down to his underwear and stepped inside the tub. He reached down and covered his body with the mixture before stepping out onto a towel and waiting for Abilio to do the same. Then, Abilio pulled the plug and rinsed himself off before trading places with his cousin.

"What now?" Jesus asked, half expecting the ritual slaughter of an animal, where he'd put his foot down and say no.

"We let the candle burn down."

"That's it?"

"That's it."

"Ok, well you're cleaning up."

"Obviously," Abilio said, rolling his eyes.

After putting the house back in order, the pair were getting ready for bed when Beatriz came home. She paused in the door-way, her nose in the air while she sniffed, and looked at Abilio with a sternness she reserved for when she meant business.

"What did I tell you about your damned magic!" she roared, crossing herself.

CHAPTER THREE

Jesus showed up for work in the morning right as the private security guard walked out the front door. They exchanged a slight nod as they passed each other, before the guard settled into his post next to the entrance. After passing through the museum's main floor, Jesus went through the double doors that had a sign warning against unauthorized personnel and made his way to the back office. There, he found Isabella already at her desk, staring at her computer screen.

After a quick knock on the open door, he stood in the doorway and said, "Good morning."

"Good morning," Isabella replied.

"Where did you want me today?"

Isabella turned her seat away from the computer and faced Jesus before beckoning him inside. "Close the door," she added, before Jesus got too far into the room.

He did as she said before approaching her desk.

"Go on, sit down," Isabella said, gesturing with pursed lips to the chair in front of her desk. She folded her hands in front of her, resting them on the desk, as Jesus took a seat.

"Santi sent me a text after he left yesterday," Isabella began.

She paused, gathering her thoughts. "Pretty much, he said he knew I would put you back at the front desk, and he wanted to make sure I didn't."

Jesus squeezed his lips together and nodded.

"Now, I know you've earned the position, but for now can you just sit tight in your old job, making sure the place stays clean? I'll see what I can do about putting you somewhere else, maybe working on the displays."

Making Isabella feel worse about the situation was the last thing Jesus wanted. He knew it wasn't her fault, that there was a chain of command that she was bound to, one with Santi entrenched at the top.

"Of course," he replied. "It's only been a few days at the front desk anyways—no big deal."

"Thank you," Isabella said with a sigh. All of a sudden, she looked up to the wall behind Jesus, as if performing mental arithmetic. "I wonder . . ."

Jesus waited a moment, until Isabella said, "That's all, for now," then he got up and left.

An uneventful morning passed by while Jesus performed his previous job's tasks—walking around and looking for trash, spills, or spots left by visitors. During the week, most of the guests were primary school students bussed in from the nearby schools, and that Tuesday was more of the same. Armed with a rag and his bottle of diluted glass cleaner, Jesus walked behind the various groups, cleaning the smudges the children left on the glass covering the displays.

Rodrigo arrived when Jesus was eating his lunch outside in the building's shade. He sat down next to Jesus and leaned his back against the smooth concrete wall.

"I'm not at the front desk anymore," Jesus said after their initial small talk.

"Really? I didn't think that was permanent."

"It wouldn't have been if it was up to Isabella, but Santi called her and made sure she didn't reverse the move."

"That guy doesn't play around," Rodrigo said, the pity clear in his voice.

"No, he doesn't."

"Oh well, it was fun while it lasted. I'll just pay." Rodrigo looked at Jesus and smirked. "And the tourists will just have to pay a bit more."

Jesus laughed. "Just make sure no one catches you."

"No way, I'm smooth, like a spy." Rodrigo relaxed his face and smoldered. "Like in the movies."

After finishing his meal, Jesus went back into the museum, telling Rodrigo that he had to wait before coming inside so they wouldn't be seen together. "I'm not getting caught up in your schemes," he said.

As soon as he walked in, the baby-faced new employee now stationed at the front desk spotted him and made a beeline towards his position.

"There's a spill near the entrance. They told me to find you," the promoted employee said with a twinge of embarrassment.

Part of Jesus felt like being rude to the young man, rolling his eyes and scoffing, but instead he nodded and said he'd go get the mop.

The spill turned out to be a dropped, exploded can of soda. Orange soda, with a large blast radius. The heavyset boy who'd dropped the drink was more upset about not having a soda for his lunch and couldn't care less about the museum's inconvenience.

Jesus, having experienced a similar situation before, was glad the kid hadn't dropped a glass bottle. The last time this happened, he'd had to get rid of the mop because he kept finding pieces of glass later that afternoon, unaware that they were hiding in the mop's fibers. After cleaning the most recent spill, he went back for a bucket of fresh hot water and mopped it once more so that visitors wouldn't find a sticky floor.

While he was rolling the mop bucket back to the closet, he saw one of a pair of men testing if the glass covering the display was locked. With a laugh, the one who pulled on the display turned to his companion and shook his head.

Jesus hurried back to the janitor's closet, put the mop bucket back inside, and grabbed his rag and window cleaner. Then, he walked back out to the exhibits and made sure he kept the suspicious pair in his sights while wiping nonexistent smudges.

Rodrigo had put the idea of a spy in his head, and Jesus, in all seriousness, acted like the archetypes he saw in his favorite movies. He studied his targets' body language and tried reading their lips, determining they were American when he heard their English words rising above the museum's background noise. They tested every piece of glass in front of the displays, finding each one locked. Of course, Jesus had a key—part of his responsibility was dusting the pieces on display when nobody was around. But there was an unspoken policy in place that he wait for Isabella's orders before going into the displays themselves, which he made sure he followed.

The tourists came to the last exhibit Jesus had opened and cleaned—weeks ago at that point. It was a statue of a Mayan man in full warrior dress. Below the statue, miniature human figures showed what a battle might have looked like between the Mayan warriors and the Spanish conquistadors. While Jesus watched, wiping the glass at the end of the hall, the bolder tourist reached his fingers around the edge of the glass and pulled.

The glass lifted up an inch before the man let go in surprise. He looked at his friend with his mouth open in excitement, and the friend nodded, urging him on.

Jesus felt his stomach drop and his legs buckle. He doubted anyone else had been inside the case since he cleaned it—opening them wasn't something the museum did often. He looked up at the camera, convinced that a quick scan through the past weeks would show that he was the last person inside the display, that he was the person who'd left it unlocked.

And, for some reason, Abilio's tarot reading echoed through his mind, at—in his opinion—the exact worst moment. A new journey.

As Jesus watched in horror, the emboldened tourist reached a hand underneath the glass, twisting his body as he did so, and grabbed one of the small figurines, part of the lower display showing a hypothetical battle centuries ago. Then, he put the glass back in place without making a sound. The smiling thief pocketed the figurine and walked towards the exit with his friend.

Although there were many small human figurines in the display case, Jesus could lose his job if the theft was ever discovered. He set his rag and bottle down and followed the pair, hoping for help from the security guard at the exit.

Except, when the pair got to the glass wall at the entrance, the guard was nowhere to be found.

The pair were outside of the building by the time Jesus found his voice. "Señor!" he called out from the entrance, rushing forward without a second thought.

Neither man turned around.

"Señor!" Jesus repeated himself. Closer now, he reached out and put a hand on the thief's shoulder.

The man looked at Jesus, shrugged, and feigned ignorance.

"Can I help you?" the man said, in English.

"You stole. Give it back," Jesus said, in Spanish. He understood much more than he spoke and used to say his tongue was broken when it came to speaking English. "Steal," he added, in

English, pointing to the man's pocket. Then, he held his hand out, palm open and facing up.

"Look, man, we don't know what you're talking about," the friend said, in English, before turning around.

"Police," Jesus said as a threat, again holding out his hand. He wished he had tried harder when learning English, but learning Spanish after learning the Mayan language first was hard enough, and he didn't have his twin's gift for languages.

The pair turned around and started walking away, and Jesus put a hand on each of their shoulders. The thief pushed him, and he stumbled back, falling after his foot got caught on the concrete.

"Shit, man, let's get out of here. I'm not trying to see the inside of a Mexican jail!" one of the pair said before they both started running.

When Jesus saw that they were getting away, he tried scrambling up and giving chase. He stumbled on his first step. Down the steps, on the side of the main road that ran in front of the museum, Calle 60, the pair waved down a bus as it was pulling away and hopped on, looking back at the defeated Jesus.

Some journey that was.

Jesus walked back into the museum, encountering the security guard coming the other way. "Where were you?" Jesus said, annoyed.

"Bathroom," the security guard replied with a grin, tapping his belly. "Feel much better now."

"I'm glad," Jesus said. With any luck, he thought, nobody would notice the missing figurine. One thing was certain, that he had no plans of bringing it up himself.

His replacement called out to him as he passed the front desk. "Isabella's looking for you," he said, putting the rag and bottle on the counter. "She found these on the floor."

Jesus snatched the supplies and made his way to her office. He stood in the doorway and said, "You wanted to see me?"

"Yes, yes, come in," she said, full of excitement.

Jesus didn't understand but did as he was told, shutting the door behind him without being asked. He hadn't been alone with Isabella in her office for weeks, and now twice in one day.

"You have your passport, right?" she asked, nodding as if she could influence his answer to the objective question.

"I do."

"Thought so, I remember you going with Hugh to Costa Rica last year."

Jesus nodded, then asked why.

"Well, you know Jorge died, right?"

"Jorge . . ." Jesus said, trailing off.

"Flaco—he's the one who recommended you to me for the job!"

"Oh, right! Yes, I heard, I'm very sorry." Flaco was Isabella's godfather, and Jesus got the job at the museum through a series of connections that started with Jesus's mother, flowed through Gloria, surged past Flaco, and finally arrived at Isabella.

"Well, I was in a bit of a bind. Jorge's funeral is tomorrow, but I'm supposed to fly to Germany late tonight."

Jesus couldn't see what any of this had to do with him.

"Germany, on official museum business."

"Ok . . ." Jesus said, still not sure where she was going with the conversation.

"Look, I feel terrible about what Santi did. And this is my way of making it up to you. We already have the ticket, I can transfer it to your name right now, and you said you have your passport. All you have to do is say yes," Isabella said, her guilt palpable.

"What do I have to do in Germany?"

"It's in Dresden, to be precise."

The city's name triggered Jesus's memory of the day before.

"One of the Mayan codices is there, and they invited us for a presentation about it. All you have to do is show up and listen—in short, be the museum's ambassador."

"How much does it cost?"

Isabella laughed. "Why won't you just say yes? It's free for you, all paid for by the museum. This way, we can still have a presence at the event, and I can go to the funeral—it'll mean a lot to Gloria."

Jesus looked down at the rag in his hand and the bottle of glass cleaner. "What time is the flight? I get off at six."

Isabella shook her head. "Oh no, no, you're leaving now. Go home, pack, and head to the airport. I'll call the airline now and get it all set up."

CHAPTER FOUR

Jesus arrived at the Dresden Airport and found a serious-looking man in a black trench coat with messy white hair holding up a sign with Isabella Canche's name written in large black letters.

"She couldn't make it, so I'm here instead," he said, in Spanish.

The German man didn't know what Jesus said and stood there, dumbfounded.

Jesus pulled out his phone and used Google Translate, typing the words in and setting the output language to German.

The man read Jesus's phone, nodded, and held up a finger while saying something Jesus couldn't understand. It was his first time hearing someone speak German in person, and he had a hard time believing anyone understood the guttural sounds. After the host made a call, complete with a copious amount of nodding, he looked at Jesus and beckoned him forward, walking away.

Jesus followed his German host and met a wave of cold air as soon as they walked outside. He hugged himself and rubbed his upper arms over his long-sleeved shirt as they walked, and he was grateful when they arrived at a black Mercedes in the parking garage. Before starting the still-warm car, the host pulled out his phone, typed, and held the screen up for Jesus.

Bienvenida a Germany.

The driver plunged into the city in the darkness of night. According to Isabella, the presentation was the following day, in the morning. But, with the time change, it was well past midnight in Germany, and Jesus realized he wouldn't have time for more than a few hours of rest before he went to the Saxon State Library, where the Dresden Codex lived.

The highways didn't seem all that different from what he expected—he did notice the clearer signage—but while driving through the city on the way to the hotel, Jesus was in awe at how wide the streets were, and how much space each building had in front of it. In downtown Merida, outside of the parks, the walls of each building went clear to the sidewalk, keeping what lay beyond hidden. In Dresden, it seemed each building wanted, and welcomed, visitors, with ample space for the numerous cars parked in front, illuminated by streetlights above.

They arrived at the Holiday Inn, and the driver parked right in front of the entrance. He met Jesus at the car's trunk and took out his suitcase. "Let's go," the driver said, in English, looking at Jesus in hopes he understood.

Jesus nodded and tilted his chin towards the entrance, which drew a thin smile from the driver.

The host and staff took care of everything, handing Jesus a key card with the room number written on the protective pamphlet. Before leaving, the driver held up his hands and showed Jesus eight fingers. "Tomorrow," he said, in English.

"Eight, tomorrow," Jesus replied in the same language. Then, they parted ways, the driver to his car and Jesus to his room, where he lay down and fell asleep with his clothes still on.

He woke up to his alarm a few hours later, showered, and

got dressed. He was waiting in the lobby with his backpack on his lap when the same driver arrived at eight with a black coat in his hand. The driver tilted his head in pleasant surprise at his charge's punctuality and smiled, holding the coat out for Jesus.

Jesus had already felt the wind whenever the lobby door opened and had resigned himself to being cold in his simple striped button-down shirt. Grateful for the driver's foresight, he put the coat on, slung the backpack over his shoulders, and followed the driver out of the hotel.

The large, square buildings Jesus saw during the drive fascinated him, as well as the clear, open spaces with manicured lawns. The people also drew his attention, walking to work on the well-lined streets. He stared at their faces, looking for a glimpse of what made Germans unique. Other than their height —they were taller, on average—they seemed to be the same mix of ages and body types as back home.

After making a U-turn, they turned into a long, thin parking lot. On their right, through a well-placed row of trees, was a massive square building made of gray stone.

"Library," the driver said, in English, pointing to the building. They parked, and the driver and Jesus walked side by side away from the car and through the sliding glass doors into the library.

Inside, they went through a wide-open lobby—the Germans loved their open spaces, Jesus decided—then, a series of private reading areas. The host kept leading him forward until they arrived in a large, high-ceilinged room with rows and rows of desks and dozens of professionals milling about. The Saxon State Library's main reading room was a master class in shades of brown, yellow lighting, and clean lines. The German host scanned the room until he spotted a group of people halfway across the space and made a beeline towards their position.

Jesus's stomach dropped when he realized who they were

walking towards. It was Hugh, his twin, laughing while talking to a group of four young men surrounding him.

"Mexico," the host said, pointing to the group as they approached.

Jesus nodded and repeated the name of the country but pronounced it as if the x was a j, and the host tried repeating the word in the same manner. Jesus smiled and patted the host on the back, appreciative of the effort.

Hugh turned towards Jesus when the pair got close. His face slackened for a brief moment before he got it under control and reverted back to his light, confident smile. For each twin, it was like looking at an alternate reality, a potentiality of what they each could look like if they traded positions. While Jesus was wearing the khaki pants he reserved for church and the bulky coat, Hugh had his typical well-fitting suit. Hugh said something in English to the rest of the group he was with then pulled Jesus away from the group.

"What are you doing here?" Hugh said in Spanish, somehow both condescending and jovial at the same time.

"Isabella sent me in her place. Flaco died, and she has to go to the funeral."

"Isabella . . . that's the girl that runs the museum in Merida, right?" Hugh knew Flaco too but didn't say anything about the death.

Jesus nodded.

Hugh started laughing. "So, instead of sending the person in charge of the museum, they send the janitor? What are you going to do, clean the codex?"

Jesus released a slow exhale, closing his eyes. Somehow, Hugh never changed. He opened them and told his twin, "I'm here representing the museum."

Hugh stifled his laughter after not getting a rise from his brother and wrapped an arm around his shoulder. "Good, good,

I'm glad you're getting to see the world! How's your English? Everyone here speaks it just fine."

"Still terrible. I never practice."

"Of course not. Well, just stick with me, I'll translate what everyone's saying."

In short, Hugh never translated anything after introducing Jesus as his brother—not even his twin. He had a wonderful time chatting, in English, with what seemed like old friends, all of them British or French or German, and also wearing well-cut suits. Jesus stood there in silence, not contributing a single word, while his German host stood a few steps behind, one eye on Jesus and one eye on the growing crowd.

At one point, one of Hugh's colleagues asked Jesus a question. With a laugh, Hugh told the man that he didn't speak anything but Spanish. "And I guess he's never heard of a coat-room before," he added, pinching Jesus's black coat.

A younger version of himself would've been embarrassed, but Jesus had realized his lack of language skills wasn't a big deal once Hugh moved away from Merida. Some people are good at fixing cars, some at helping people, but nobody can be good at everything at all times.

Yelling from one side of the reading room drew everyone's attention. The woman projecting her voice said something in German, then in English, and finished with a wave of her hand.

Hugh let his friends walk ahead of him before following alongside Jesus. "The presentation is about to begin," he said, in Spanish. To Jesus, it sounded like Hugh changed his accent to sound more like he came from Spain—100 percent something his twin would do.

A nagging question crept into Jesus's head as they walked, and he asked Hugh about their mother. "Mom said you called her the other day," he said, not sure which day it was after his extensive travel.

"I did."

"Were you already here?"

"Yeah, but I found out about an open space for a store from my friend in real estate. She's being so stubborn about staying in Merida, I thought it might change her mind."

"She won't leave."

"Not when she has to take care of you and our cousin!" Hugh said with a smile, as if the dig was yet another joke.

Jesus noticed that his twin didn't even say Abilio's name and wondered if it had anything to do with Abilio's sexual orientation.

"Why do you even care about her being in Mexico City? Go ahead, move on to bigger and better and leave her alone."

Hugh put his arm around Jesus for a second time. "Listen. At some point, she won't be able to work at her little fruit stand. You don't make enough money, and neither does her new son. So, who do you think is going to pay for her living expenses? Me. And I'm not going to send money to Merida just so she can waste it on you two."

Jesus ripped himself away from Hugh's grasp.

"Look, brother, I'm just looking towards the future. And, at this rate, I'll be the one giving her grandchildren . . ." Hugh paused, studying his twin.

Jesus looked down at his feet as they walked. There was the occasional woman in his life, but it wasn't a priority for him. His mother understood and didn't bother him about it, having learned from her fruit that everything ripened in its own time.

"See? Still no women for you. And definitely no women for Abilio." The way Hugh spit out their cousin's name sent a protective surge through Jesus, and he understood why dogs snarled when threats got too close.

The two of them walked into an auditorium. On the stage in front, surrounded by glass and sitting on plush velvet, was a tattered pad of brown sheets with black markings: the Dresden Codex. A quick look around proved what Jesus suspected: out of everyone in the room, the only ones who could claim Mayan heritage were him and his brother. Something about the situation rankled him, like an eyelash caught in his eye that he couldn't get out. Not painful, but annoying, and making concentrating on anything else difficult.

The seats closest to the front were almost full, and Hugh's friends had saved him a seat near them in a prime location. Just one seat, as if Jesus hadn't been standing with them moments before. Jesus slowed down before Hugh noticed the situation, saying that he was going to sit with his host. "I'll see you after the talk," he said.

Hugh shrugged and kept walking, shaking hands with an older man with a cane on his way to his saved seat.

Jesus sat down in the less-full seats near the back of the auditorium. His host sat down with a seat between them until Jesus pushed the empty seat down and patted it, signaling to the host that he should sit down next to him. The German man smiled and changed seats, folding his hands in his lap while waiting for the presentation.

The same lady who yelled at them in the reading room walked onstage. The crowd became quiet, and she started talking, in English, beginning by thanking everyone for attending before she moved on to the Dresden Codex. A screen descended from the ceiling behind her and displayed a series of charts and graphs while she went on about their most recent discoveries.

Jesus knew enough English that he could've followed along just fine—with some help from Google Translate—but he couldn't shake the slow pressure building within his chest. All those people, with all their money, staring at something stolen from his ancestors. One of four existing examples, the rest wiped out by an overzealous Catholic during his mini-inquisition.

The Dresden Codex should be in Mexico. They all should be in Mexico.

Jesus balled his fists and closed his eyes. A focus on his breathing didn't calm him down. He cursed Hugh for putting him into this headspace before opening his eyes and finding his twin in the crowd, whispering to his giggling friends and not paying attention.

All of a sudden, he felt his nose running. He put a hand up to his nostrils, pulled them away, and found them covered in blood. Standing up in a hurry, he grabbed his backpack and rushed through the main aisle while keeping his blood from hitting the ground.

He didn't notice the sudden whispers that erupted throughout the room, and he was confused when he heard a scream coming from the speaker onstage as he walked through the auditorium doors.

"The codex!" the presenting woman said. "It's gone!"

CHAPTER FIVE

JESUS HURRIED to the bathroom as private security guards ran past him on their way to the auditorium. He set his backpack on the ground in front of the sink. After rinsing his hands and face, he left the water running and stared at himself in the mirror as the blood—thinner now because of the drops of water left above his lips—trickled past his mouth and down his chin. He wiped once more and pinched his nostrils, squeezing a bit more blood from his nose, before shuffling into a stall and grabbing a handful of toilet paper, mindful of not leaving blood on any surface. With the toilet paper, he wiped the lower half of his face before holding the wad up to his nose.

He tilted his head back and tasted iron in the back of his mouth. When was the last time he'd had a nosebleed? As a kid, maybe. Even then, it was because he'd been hit in the face when Hugh threw an orange at him when he wasn't paying attention, not this random dam burst.

After pulling the toilet paper away from his face, he looked down and stared at the dark red stain on the bright white tissue; he tilted his head back again when he felt a trickle of liquid inside his nose. While staring at the ceiling, he made his way back to the stall and grabbed more toilet paper. Back at the mirror, he pulled the wad away from his face and ripped the new toilet paper into two pieces, twisting them and shoving them into each nostril. Then, he wiped down the counter where he had set down the bloodied wad and threw everything away.

After making sure the counter was dry, he leaned his back-side against the ledge and waited. Without the urgency of dealing with dripping blood, he wondered about the last words he'd heard from the presenting woman.

The codex was gone? Was the statement part of her presen-tation, and was anything lost in translation? After thinking about it, her scream did seem out of character. And where did the codex go, with everyone watching it?

Assuming the blood had stopped, Jesus pulled the two wads from his nostrils and inspected the coagulated blood. He took two slow, small breaths, checking if there was anything left inside his nose. Confident the ordeal was over, he threw the two plugs away, washed and dried his hands, and grabbed another wad of toilet paper and shoved it into his pocket, just in case.

He picked up his backpack and slung it over his shoulders before hurrying back to the auditorium, embarrassed and hoping nobody there judged his museum because he'd left the presentation for so long.

Except, when he turned the corner onto the hall that led to the auditorium, he came face-to-face with a team of security guards outside the main doors.

An older guard barked at him, in German, while holding an open hand up, and when he stopped but made no sign that he understood, one of them, a younger man, stepped forward and spoke in English.

"Stay back," he said, waving Jesus away. "Nobody can go in."

Jesus had taken out his phone so he could translate, "I was inside," when he saw a text from his brother.

He backed away and opened the message. "Where are you?" his brother asked him, in Spanish.

"I went to the bathroom and they won't let me back in," Jesus said, via text.

The bubbles that showed his brother was typing appeared right away.

"Host said your nose was bleeding."

"It's done now."

"The codex disappeared all of a sudden. You're lucky you got out, this could take a while."

"Should I go back to the hotel?"

The bubbles appeared, then went away. Jesus looked at the security guards. One of them, the one who'd spoken to him in German, was watching him with suspicious eyes while the rest of the men and women in the group of guards talked amongst themselves.

Jesus's phone vibrated. "The host said he'll call a car for you." He turned around while reading the message and started walking towards the entrance.

At the same moment, the German-speaking guard started in his direction, ready for a confrontation about why the young man was sticking around. When he saw Jesus back away, he returned to the auditorium's doors, locking down the room with a scowl on his face until the Dresden city detectives arrived.

A black Mercedes, identical to the car he rode in earlier, pulled into the parking lot and slowed down in front of Jesus. The passenger-side window rolled down and a man—who looked like a version of the host who'd made a few different life-style decisions over the years—leaned over and asked if he was Jesus. He spoke the name as an English-speaker would.

Jesus nodded, and the host tilted his head towards the back

seat. Jesus got in and set his backpack down on the seat next to him.

While Jesus's first German driver was thin and wiry, this one was broad and had the look of someone who knew his way around a gym, like he could have been private security for a celebrity or did it during his off-hours. Instead of leaving his hair messy, the new driver combed his white hair straight back. Other than those two obvious differences, the two men looked the same, with the same serious bearing and wrinkles around their eyes. In fact, while they were driving the ten minutes back to the Holiday Inn, Jesus saw the man look at him in the rearview mirror and got the sense he was looking at a twin.

Jesus, not confident in his English and still preoccupied with the events that had transpired at the library, didn't engage the driver in conversation. When he got dropped off at the Holiday Inn, he said, "Thank you," walked in, and went straight to his room. He took off his backpack and threw it onto his bed.

Something about the way his backpack plopped down piqued his curiosity. He had brought a notepad and pen, plus his personal belongings, and his bag should have rolled a bit, or bent, because his notepad didn't have a hard cover. Instead, the bag stayed flat and seemed to sink into the bed, as if there was a heavy weight inside. Jesus lifted one side of his backpack, didn't feel much extra weight, then set it down again, watching as it sunk into the mattress to a peculiar depth.

Jesus unzipped the top and almost fell over before opening his bag all the way. Inside, peeking through the opening, was black writing on old paper. No, ancient paper, and more like fabric. The Mayan writing seemed more worn than the replica he saw in the Merida museum, and he assumed the script he saw on a regular basis back home was one of the better-preserved parts of the document. He stared at the script as a surge of pride and anger welled within him. Pride, at being descended from the people who made the document, and anger, that an upset Catholic burned the rest during an unsanctioned inquisition.

"No, no, no," Jesus said as the magnitude of the situation dawned on him. He thought about the security guards locking down the auditorium, in particular the one stern-looking man who first approached him. And, the more Jesus thought about it, those were just the ones responsible for locking down the room —he had no idea what kind of German superhumans were coming from the city, what they would do to him if they found out he had the codex.

But he hadn't done anything! All that happened was his nosebleed, and he walked out. How did the codex get into his bag in the first place?

Jesus thought back to Abilio and his Santeria. Blood magic. He wasn't sure how the pieces fit together, but he was sure his cousin had something to do with it. After hearing Jesus was going on an adventure, had Abilio cast a spell to make him a thief? There wasn't any money coming his way from a stolen codex—who would buy something that came with a massive target?

The realization that he believed in Santeria, that he had even a trickle of faith in his cousin's magic, made Jesus sit down on the bed next to the open backpack. He looked down at the codex before zipping his backpack up, worried about exposing the ancient document to the air. He'd seen and heard enough about artifact preservation from Isabella to know not to touch the pages with his hands because of the oils.

Jesus lay all the way down with his hands behind his head. He alternated between staring at the ceiling and out the window as the day dragged on, deciding what he should do about his situation. For one, he didn't like the idea of getting in trouble for stealing the codex when he never stole it in the first place—it just appeared in his backpack! But he knew nobody would listen; they'd want facts and details about how he'd carried it out before locking him away for a very long time. Walking the Mayan document back to the library wasn't an option.

And why would it be? It was written by his ancestors. If anyone should have it, it should be him, and the museum in Merida. Back where it belonged, in the land where it was written.

The more Jesus thought about it, the more he thought the situation might turn out well for him. Wasn't Santi just saying the other day how the codices should be back in Mexico? His thoughts then trailed back to Abilio and his spell for more money. Well, if Jesus brought the codex back, maybe there would be a new job for him at the museum, one with a raise and a hefty dose of respect.

One thing was certain—the backpack, and the codex, couldn't leave his sight. And to be extra safe, he decided he would stay in his hotel room until his flight back to Merida the following evening.

With help from the hotel staff, he ordered food from a Greek restaurant across the street and had it delivered, showing up in the lobby with his backpack on and scurrying back to his room with his food in hand. He didn't respond to texts from Hugh, but he did find out that the guests weren't allowed out of the auditorium until late that afternoon, after they were all interviewed. His host called twice, and Jesus ignored them both times before sending a text saying, "What time for the airport tomorrow?"

The host responded with a simple, "Four," and Jesus didn't hear from him again until then.

With his ride outside the hotel, Jesus fit what small items he could inside his backpack's front pockets and put the rest into his suitcase. Under normal circumstances, he would have kept more of his belongings in his carry-on for the plane ride, but he didn't want anything else in the largest pocket alongside the codex. In fact, he didn't want the pocket opened at all.

As it turned out, he wasn't so lucky.

After the host dropped a distracted Jesus off at the airport, Jesus checked his bag with a fair amount of help from his phone for translation. Then, he followed the signs to the security station. After waiting in line, Jesus put his backpack and shoes on the conveyor belt, watching as the codex went through the X-ray machine before he went through the metal detector.

Jesus watched the guard who looked at every item that passed through the conveyor belt. He stared at Jesus's shoes first, then furrowed his brow when he saw the backpack on the screen. Jesus's heart fluttered, and he wondered if the entire city knew about the missing museum piece. The guard's hand hovered over a button near his workstation for a moment before he committed to stopping the conveyor belt. Another guard pulled the bin holding Jesus's backpack and took it to a separate area. She said something in German, then, when Jesus showed no sign of comprehension, she said, in English, "Is this your bag?"

Jesus nodded, his heart racing. The hand holding his phone was slick with sweat.

"Come with me." She pointed to his shoes, and he grabbed them. Before Jesus could put them on, she beckoned him to a stainless steel table.

"Open it," she commanded, holding the backpack out. To his relief, she had on blue latex gloves.

With trembling hands, Jesus unzipped his backpack and showed her the contents.

"For reading?" she said, laughing, reaching in and moving

the ancient document forward and backward with a light touch, looking around it for anything noteworthy.

Jesus typed into his phone for a translation. "Replica," he said aloud, happy the word was the same as in his native language, just missing an accent mark.

"Looks like it belongs in a museum," the guard said in accented English. She looked at Jesus, a picture of seriousness while studying his face, then zipped up the backpack and handed it over. "Have a good trip," she said, turning back to the rest of the waiting travelers and waving forward the next person in line.

CHAPTER SIX

JESUS SPENT the trip from Dresden to Merida second-guessing his decision. What was he thinking, carrying a stolen artifact back to Mexico? His nervousness, combined with the lengthy flights and layovers, left the dampness under his arms smelling sharp, worse than he could ever remember. He felt bad for the well-dressed woman sitting next to him as the plane descended into Merida, and he kept his arms close to his body as much as he could.

He held his breath while passing through customs, and again when he went through the agricultural checkpoint after collecting his bag. The guards waved him through with little fanfare, since he didn't have any tobacco or fruit, and the dogs that sniffed him continued on to other travelers without hesitation.

Walking through the automatic sliding doors into the Mexican sunshine sent a surge of gratitude through his bones. He stood in the sunlight with his face to the sky, thankful that he made it back without getting caught and feeling like the next chapter of his life was about to start.

The new journey Abilio saw in the cards. Jesus the fool,

standing there with a priceless piece of Mayan culture brought back home.

He started walking towards the street that ran past the airport and grabbed a bus towards El Centro instead of hailing one of the overpriced cabs outside the terminal. He kept the backpack on his knees while he rode, his eyes watching his fellow travelers, wondering how they would react if they knew the accidental heist he had pulled off. Part of him wanted the adulation, and part of him wanted the anonymity that came with involving Santi. After one more bus transfer, he arrived a few blocks from his house and walked the rest of the way home to an empty house, since Abilio and Beatriz were busy at the fruit stand.

Jesus set his backpack on the bed and began unpacking his suitcase. Every few moments, he would look at the bag and chuckle to himself, wondering what on Earth he was thinking and grateful he could play a part in bringing a part of Mayan history back home. After one of the quickest showers he had ever taken—since he didn't want the bag out of his sight for long—he came back out, got dressed again, and sat down on the bed next to his bag.

"Might as well have a look," he said out loud. He unzipped the bag and looked at the Dresden Codex in awe. Knowing the need for hand protection, he took the pillowcases off of the two pillows on his bed and slipped his arms inside. Then, he withdrew the codex and held it in his hands.

The pages were the size of a large pocket travel guide— maybe a small tablet—and were folded accordion-style. Jesus pulled the top sheet and looked at the pages below, wondering what information his ancestors had saved for their people. Unlike his twin, he had given up on higher education a long time ago, but he felt a call deep in his bones for a potential future where he learned what the individual characters meant so that he could read them and pass down the knowledge for future generations. He spent a long time flipping through and staring at the pages, hoping that somehow the meaning would become apparent through osmosis—he came from the same people as the author, after all. Every so often, he looked at the room around him, searching for movement, a shadow, or a light that indicated the person who wrote the document was in the room with him, had survived through the ages via their words.

Night had descended on the city by the time he put the codex back into his backpack, took the pillowcases off of his hands, and put the backpack underneath the bed he shared with Abilio. The museum was closed, and he had no other way of getting in touch with Santi—his triumphant return would have to wait until the next day. He got a head start on cooking dinner, so his mother could come home and relax for once instead of continuing with still more tasks after working all day.

Abilio and Beatriz strolled into their home and found dinner waiting for them. After a round of welcome-back hugs and greetings, they sat down together at the table and ate while Jesus told them all about his trip, including how he saw Hugh and a thorough description of Germany. He told them about the missing codex but left out the part where it had appeared in his backpack. There also wasn't any mention of staying in his room for a day instead of going out and sightseeing in the foreign city.

Jesus made sure Abilio wasn't alone in the room without him, but since Beatriz was still in the house the entire evening, there was no reason for his cousin to go beneath the bed for his box of magic supplies and find the backpack. Still, by the time everyone in the house went to bed, Jesus was tired of worrying about the potential discovery and couldn't wait for the next morning, when he could start the new chapter of his life as the man who brought the codex back to the Yucatán, even if it was only Santi and maybe Isabella who would know.

That night, Jesus dreamed for the first time in recent memory. He was at Cenote X'batun—the one he and his friends went to most often for a swim—but this time, he was alone. He was in his underwear, treading water while holding on to the limestone rock surrounding the natural pool, when he saw a dark purple jaguar with black spots appear at the edge of the water and take a drink. The animal looked like it was made from the night, and it kept its large yellow eyes on him while it lapped water. All of a sudden, it turned around and walked away with a swish of its tail . . .

Jesus opened his eyes and found himself back in his room, his heart beating fast. Taking slow, deep breaths, he sat up and looked at the door. There, he thought he saw the small movement of a tail leaving the room in the dim light. He threw the sheet off of himself and got out of bed.

Abilio, sensing the movement, groaned and rearranged himself. Jesus froze and waited until his cousin lay still once more. Then, he tiptoed out of the bedroom and went into the main room. He looked around for signs of movement, searching in the stillness of night, and moved to get a better view of the side of the house farthest from the street. Believing his mind had played tricks on him, he started back towards his room when he saw it: an unmistakable purple tail, as thick as his forearm, disappearing through the door that led to their backyard. Jesus hurried after the beast, making sure his footfalls made no sounds, and peeked out through the door with just his head so that he could make a quick exit back into the house if necessary, not realizing that solid materials hadn't stopped the creature yet.

There, in his backyard, the same purple jaguar sat underneath the lime tree, his tail lying on the ground around him. The large yellow orbs in his face stared at Jesus.

"It's ok, Jesus," the jaguar said, his voice deep and powerful. "I'm here to thank you."

Jesus's curiosity overrode his fear and he stepped outside. "Thank me?" he said, approaching the animal made from the night's darkness.

The jaguar's massive jaws came up to Jesus's waist. "Yes, thank you. You brought enough power back to this land for me to walk the Earth again."

Jesus shook his head in disbelief. "Wait, what?" He looked around his backyard, wondering if he was still dreaming. The fruit trees were still bare—what fruit had sprouted had already been plucked by his mother—and he could hear cars in the distance. Black marks from a long-ago fire stained the concrete. But, there was no ignoring the purple jaguar sitting in front of him. It seemed like a dark shadow without a clear source of light, with fuzzy edges that blended into the surrounding darkness.

"Perhaps I should start at the beginning," the jaguar said. "My name is Balam."

Jesus stifled a laugh. There were dozens of little shops around Merida that capitalized on the Mayan word for "jaguar," and he decided his mind was playing tricks on him inside of a dream. Well, he might as well play along.

"Ok, Balam. What power are you talking about?"

"The power in the codex underneath your bed."

Jesus's stomach dropped, and he took a shallow breath.

"A long time ago, there were twelve head priests at the city of Chichen Itza." A series of shadow buildings surrounding the main pyramid, the Temple of Kukulcán, appeared on the ground in front of the jaguar. The image zoomed in and showed twelve men standing in front of the steps of the massive pyramid, next to the head of the shadow serpent that appears on the equinoxes.

"The codices both preserved them and gave them their power. They had everything about their civilization written down: farming, astronomy, construction techniques, and the origin of life—"

"But Chichen Itza was abandoned," Jesus said.

Balam turned his attention from the shadows on the ground in front of him and stared at Jesus. When faced with the yellow orbs, Jesus turned his lips inward and squeezed them together.

The purple jaguar continued. "Everything was good, until they ran into a problem—the priests couldn't agree on the best use of their magic. A typical human problem, in hindsight, and one that should have been planned for. In essence, they arranged themselves into four factions: to share their magic with everyone, to use it to gain power and land, to condense the ruling priesthood to one man, and to only use magic for protection."

"Some of the priests wanted to give up their magic so one guy could have it all?"

"They were scared of a prophesied invader and thought a single decision-maker could fare better than their bloated group."

The twelve priests in the shadow display disappeared, and four groups of three men appeared, one on each side of the pyramid. They walked away from the four faces of the temple and disappeared into the surrounding jungle. "The four factions split up around one thousand years ago, leaving Chichen Itza to the jungle. Each of them took one-fourth of their writings, enough power for them all, but no longer centralized."

The plants surrounding the city overtook the buildings. "The Spaniard Montejo, when he arrived, learned about the codices and heard rumors of their power. He looked for signs of the Mayan magic while in the Yucatán, losing many nights of sleep, and the priests in charge of the codices kept their gifts hidden as long as they could. He did manage to steal three, sending them to Europe and hoping the scholars could unlock their secrets, but without any connection to the land, the documents lay inert."

"What about the ones who wanted to gain power, or use the magic for protection? Why didn't they use their magic against the Spanish?"

"The Spaniards were tricky. They made alliances and promises with the Maya, so the priests thought they were safe. In essence, each group thought they'd be the ones who were spared until it was too late."

Balam rendered a new shadow image. The overgrown temple disappeared in a swirl of purple, and from the darkness emerged a miniature group of distraught Maya surrounding a large fire in the middle of a town. Bald men in long robes watched the flames while holding up a different book: the Bible.

"Then, one man burned every codex he could find. What nobody suspected, or realized, was that instead of destroying the magic in the codices, he condensed it. The single codex that survived in the Yucatán provided enough power for the continuation of Mayan culture—which is why there are so many proud Maya today. But, it wasn't until you brought back the second that there was enough power for me to reemerge from the shadow realm."

The shadow image of the massive fire disappeared, to Jesus's relief. Watching his ancestors mourn the loss of their relics hit him harder than expected.

"And you, where do you fit into all of this?"

"Think of me as a guide. In fact, it was your ancestor that awakened me in the first place, the night before the summer solstice," Balam said, dropping his chin.

Jesus thought he detected a hint of pride in the jaguar, even though it was his first time reading the facial expressions of a cat.

The shadow image of the four groups walking away from

Chichen Itza reappeared, and the image zoomed all the way down onto one man.

Jesus leaned forward and inspected the small shadow man, ignoring the fact that he left the back of his neck exposed to the jaguar. "Which group did he belong to?" Jesus asked.

"He wanted to share the magic with everyone, so all Maya could have a piece."

Jesus found himself relieved. He thought of Hugh and guessed his twin would prefer being a member of the group wanting power and land.

"How was he going to do it?" Jesus said, looking at Balam.

"There's only one way: bury all the codices inside the main temple at Chichen Itza, the Temple of Kukulcán."

"But they were already at Chichen Itza before . . ." Jesus replied.

"The other priests didn't want their power reduced, so they never initiated the ritual."

Jesus nodded. "Too bad the other two are still in Europe," he said, crestfallen.

"I know. It's up to you to bring them back."

Jesus put his hands up and backed away. "Wait. No, wait. I almost got in major trouble getting this one here. And you're saying I need to bring two more? No way, I can't do it!"

The lights snapped on inside the house, throwing thin rays onto the backyard. Where the light hit him, Balam appeared as a small black house cat, but in the night, he still maintained his purple jaguar form. It was a strange image, alternating streaks of different-sized cats. He slinked away, jumping onto the concrete wall surrounding the property.

"Jesus!" Beatriz yelled from the back door. "What are you doing outside?"

CHAPTER SEVEN

JESUS WOKE up the next morning, a Sunday, convinced that the entire ordeal with Balam had been a figment of his dreaming imagination. Hadn't he been tired from his long flight from Germany to Mexico? His guilty mind was playing tricks on him, that's all. He brushed his teeth, catching his reflection in the mirror and laughing at his gullibility. There was no way a jaguar from his dreams appeared in his backyard. And a conversation with him? Forget about it.

Beatriz didn't mention the discovery of her son in the back-yard, and that added fuel to his conviction. She set his plate of eggs, rice, and beans in front of her son—the second plate of food on the table—and asked him if his cousin was still in bed.

Jesus nodded as he grabbed a fork and started eating. His mother marched to the bedroom.

"Wake up," she said.

Jesus imagined Abilio rolling over and surrounding himself with the sheet.

"I said, wake up!" Beatriz repeated with a sterner tone.

"Okay, okay, I'm up," Abilio conceded. He appeared in the

main room wrapped in his white sheet, followed by Beatriz, then sat down in front of his plate.

"Back to work today?" Beatriz asked Jesus while she took fresh tortillas from the stove. She set them on the table before returning and cracking two eggs for her own breakfast.

"That's the plan. Isabella said it was fine if I got there a little late today, since I was traveling yesterday."

"Then why are you up now?" Abilio asked with his mouth full. His puffy eyes stayed focused on his plate.

"Because this is when we get up," Beatriz said.

"Might as well get back into the swing of things," Jesus added. "I'll just head over at the normal time—" He paused while he collected his thoughts. "I need to tell them about my trip."

In reality, he wanted the codex gone. The guilt of having the priceless artifact had already inspired bad dreams, and the sooner he got rid of the document the sooner he could get some of the money Abilio's spell promised.

"Maybe there are more trips in your future, now that they see how well you handled this one," Beatriz said, chopping up the eggs in the pan.

Jesus didn't reply. He was lost in thought, wondering why he kept believing in Abilio's magic but couldn't believe that magic from his ancestors had created a shadow jaguar. He shook his head, deciding that believing in either type of magic was a recipe for disappointment. And damnation.

Halfway through his meal, Abilio reached over and grabbed his phone from where he left it on the counter the night before.

"That's weird," he said, perking up. "I didn't put it on the charger, but it says my battery's at one hundred percent."

"Huh," Beatriz replied, uninterested, a simple noise that recognized her adopted son had spoken. She scooped the eggs from the pan onto a plate and started eating standing up.

Abilio shrugged and started scrolling.

Neither of them noticed Jesus's vacant stare while he contemplated the oddity. He had heard of wireless chargers, and had thought about buying one for himself, but he couldn't shake the sense that there was power coursing through the house that had charged Abilio's phone. And if there was, he thought he might know where the power was coming from . . .

The Dresden Codex, hidden under his bed. But did that also mean Balam existed and was right about the power in the Mayan writing? And why couldn't he feel an extra source of power in the house? If there was, Abilio should be wide awake. Jesus brushed the occurrence off as random, reached for a tortilla, and took a bite.

Beatriz gathered the dishes when they all finished eating, took them to the sink, and started cleaning while her two boys got ready for the day. Once she was done, she stepped into the backyard to check what fruit she could gather from her own trees, so she could buy less at the market.

"Boys, come out here!" she exclaimed.

Jesus and Abilio hurried to the backyard and found the matriarch on her knees, hands folded in front of her face in prayer. In front of her, the lime and black sapote trees hung heavy with fruit.

They had been barren the night before, Jesus knew, or at least they had been in what he assumed was a dream.

She thanked God many times and crossed herself before standing up.

"Help me pick all this fruit!" she said, beaming with happiness.

Jesus looked at the concrete walls that surrounded their backyard, searching for a black house cat. He thought he saw movement on the wall closest to the house, but his mother pushed him back towards the house before he could investigate further.

"Get the baskets," she said.

Jesus walked back out with various-sized containers, small ones for people who wanted the actual fruit, and large ones for the fruit they would use for the smoothies they made at the fruit stand. Under normal circumstances, the best and largest pieces of fruit would go into the smaller baskets, and the misshapen and blemished fruit would go into the large baskets for further processing. But, that morning, every piece of fruit was perfect, well-formed and blemish-free. And, in reality, there was so much of the two types that Beatriz, Abilio, and Jesus just kept picking, putting it wherever there was space. They had to be careful with the black sapote, also called the chocolate pudding fruit, because of its softness; Beatriz made sure Abilio stayed far away from its harvest, knowing his propensity for tossing fruit into the baskets.

"A miracle from God! I'll have to thank him today at church," Beatriz said when they were finished filling the baskets. There was still more fruit on the trees, but there wasn't any room left in their containers.

Jesus had another idea of why the fruit grew, and it didn't have to do with God. He had trouble believing it, but after seeing the barren trees the night before and the difference in the morning, he had no choice but to face the truth: that the codex under his bed did more than he first imagined.

Jesus lingered in the backyard when Beatriz and Abilio went back inside. He waited until a small black cat appeared from behind the roof, walked along the concrete wall, sat down, and stared at him. The yellow eyes were the same ones he remembered and seemed too large for the cat's face.

"You're real, aren't you," Jesus whispered.

Balam nodded.

"And the power from the codex made the fruit grow?"

Another nod.

Jesus put his hands on his head and started pacing. He paused outside the back door and looked inside at the big smile on his mother's face. "She's so happy," he said, more to himself than to Balam.

The cat jumped from the wall onto a nearby branch, continuing down until he was on the ground. Jesus approached him—part of him still wary of an unknown cat—and sat down with his back against the lime tree, facing his home. The cat walked over and paced near Jesus's hand until he lifted it, then the cat walked underneath so Jesus petted the length of his spine. He sat down next to Jesus, facing away from the house.

"The plants hear the call," Balam said. "That's how Montejo eventually found the writing when he came over from Europe—he burned entire tracts of land where he thought the codices could be then watched where the plants grew back overnight."

"Will bringing back the magic keep the plants growing like this?"

Balam forced air out from his small cat body, and Jesus realized it was a chuckle. "After they're buried in the temple? It depends. The magic shows up differently for different people. Some of the priests did have ripe hands—"

"Ripe hands?"

"Fruit or flowers appeared on any plants they touched."

Jesus paused, thinking. "The magic isn't spells? I thought that's what was written on the codices."

"No, no, it's not like the book of spells your young cousin keeps hidden under the mattress. There aren't any spells—the codices just tell about the Mayan way of life, so the author can live forever and future generations can benefit from their knowledge." Balam paused, then sighed. "That's why the book burning was so traumatic, so many lives up in flames for no reason, gone from this world forever."

"Then how did the codices give them magic?" Jesus asked, confused.

"The codices held the entire Mayan way of life inside them, everything the culture was, but the physical pages were also the connection to the shadow realm. With the codices, each priest could connect to their shadow form and bring forth their magic. There were ripe hands, and healers—"

"Wait, so do I have a shadow form?"

"Yes, you do."

Jesus looked around. His own shadow was on the ground to his right.

"It's not quite the same," Balam said, noticing Jesus's gaze. "There's another plane of existence, layered on the one you're used to, that's connected to the rest of the world. Plants and animals experience both but, without consciousness, have no knowledge that they do. I was a normal jaguar cub captured by your ancestor before he woke me up. My physical form passed from the Earth long ago, but my shadow form still exists."

"How are you sitting here then, if you don't have a physical form?" Jesus petted the cat again. "I can feel you."

"Your shadow's the one touching me and seeing me, passing on the sensations to your physical body."

"So they can't see you?" Jesus said, tilting his chin towards the house and referring to his mother and cousin.

"Oh, they can, and so can everyone else, but it's their shadow forms that interact with me, interpreted by their senses. For all intents and purposes, I exist."

"Ok," Jesus said, unconvinced. "What's my shadow form like? Is it just me, but dark purple?"

"Not quite," Balam said. Something in his voice gave Jesus the sense that the cat was keeping some secret hidden from him.

"Well . . . ?"

"It's the same dark, rich purple, but let's just say . . . it's been neglected," Balam said. He hurried to offer more context. "Let's put it this way—you know how exercise makes someone big and strong?"

"Yes," Jesus said with trepidation.

"Ok, since they don't operate with physical constraints, a shadow form can become much larger than the physical form."

"Got it. So mine's tiny?"

"No, it's still about your height. But, since you never use your gift, your shadow form is thin. Very thin, and looks sick." Balam turned his entrancing eyes towards Jesus. "It could be worse. Without any connection to the land, many people's shadows wither until they are little more than a thin wisp trailing behind their physical form."

"Wait, what's my gift? I've never done anything magical before."

"You haven't? How did you get the codex into your bag?" Even though Balam's voice wasn't as powerful as Jesus remembered from the night before, the caring wisdom shone through.

"I don't know. I just got a nosebleed and rushed out—the next thing I knew, it was in my bag."

"The nosebleed came from all of the misplaced power in the codex; without plants and animals around, it builds up in those who still have a decent connection with their shadow. You bled because of the magic, unleashing more power."

"Fine, but how did the codex end up in my bag? What's my power?"

"You can teleport objects. In essence, you collapse the space in the shadow realm between two points, and non-sentient objects can pass through to you. Others' shadows can move objects too, but the movement shows up in the real world, instead of teleportation."

Jesus laid his head back against the tree. "Can you teach me to control it?"

Balam sighed. "Of course, but anything you learn now just scratches the surface of what you can do once you have the rest of the codices here."

"So I need to bring the rest back to really access my powers," Jesus said, nodding. "And there's a chance they'd have powers too?" he asked Balam, pointing inside his house.

The black cat turned and looked at the house with Jesus. Together, they heard Beatriz tell Abilio how they were going to make a lot of money that day.

"She could have ripe hands, or I could see her being a healer. There's only one way to find out . . ."

"Get all the codices, bring them to Chichen Itza, and bury them in the temple."

"On the equinox," Balam added.

"The equinox! That's in a few weeks!"

"It's the only way to spread the magic to everyone."

Jesus thought about his mother, about how different her life would be without worrying about buying all of her fruit from the market. And how she'd never have to rely on Hugh for anything, no matter what happened. He set his jaw and turned to Balam.

"I'll do it."

CHAPTER EIGHT

"How was your trip?" Isabella said, looking up from her computer after Jesus walked into her office.

Jesus sat down in the chair on the opposite side of the desk. Before he could answer her question, Isabella stood up, walked to the door, and closed it without making a sound.

"I heard the codex went missing when you were there," she said.

Jesus had his statement prepared. "I was in the bathroom and got blocked from going back into the auditorium. There were guards everywhere, speaking angry German," he said, making the story as interesting as possible.

He didn't mention the codex's sudden appearance in his backpack, or how he'd smuggled it back into Mexico.

"Wow, what a trip that turned out to be!" Isabella leaned in close. "Did you see anyone you think did it?"

"There were a few suspicious characters," Jesus said, feeding her curiosity. She loved true crime shows, and being one step removed from a heist inspired the thrill of a hunt.

"What'd they look like," she said, enthralled.

Jesus described the driver who picked him up from the

library. "Bulky guy, white slicked-back hair—much too big for a library worker. He's my main suspect."

Isabella leaned back and stared at the ceiling. "Did you tell the detectives?"

Although Jesus never mentioned the detectives, Isabella was familiar enough with the process that she knew about their necessary involvement. "I mentioned it to one of the guards. I assume they took it from there," he said.

Isabella leaned back, digesting the information. "Other than that, how was Germany? Did you like it?" she asked.

"What I saw? Of course. Very nice. Spacious."

"That's what I hear."

They both paused then started talking at the same time.

"So for today—" Isabella said.

"I was wondering—" said Jesus.

They both laughed when they stopped talking.

"You first," Isabella said, dropping her chin.

"Well, I was curious about seeing the other codices. Now that one of them is missing, there's no telling how long the others will still be around."

Isabella brightened. "It's funny you say that! Santi called me last night and said essentially the same thing."

"Oh? Does he usually call you on the weekends?"

"God no, this was the first time it happened in a while. But he said he was inspired. He wants me to go and see the Madrid and Paris codices in person." Isabella sat up tall and tilted her face back so she was looking down her nose at Jesus. She deepened her voice: "'You are in charge of a Mayan culture museum,' he said."

Jesus sighed. "There's no way I can go see them too . . ." He looked her in the eye. "Or is there?"

Isabella returned to her normal posture and leaned back in her chair. "I don't know . . . He made a comment about the cost, so I don't think he'd be too happy with paying for another flight. And the plan is for me to leave tomorrow—that's a quick turn-around for you."

In a flash of inspiration, Jesus made a show of looking around before leaning forward. "Well, I was thinking: What if someone wants to steal the Madrid Codex too? I was there at Dresden, I could see if I recognize anyone, or see the man with the white hair again . . ." Then, he shook his head. "No, no, what are the chances? It's a dumb idea."

"No, you might be onto something!" Isabella exclaimed. "If there's a thief going after the codices, we need to find them. Imagine the press the museum would get." Her brown eyes glossed over. "Merida museum finds thief and returns codices," she said, uttering the potential future headline.

"But Santi. He's not exactly a fan of me."

"Yes, he wasn't too happy when he found out you went instead of me. But I explained to him that I had a funeral that I couldn't miss, and that since you weren't needed at the front desk anymore, it made sense that you went."

"He probably won't be happy to hear you're trying to get another ticket for me."

"Maybe. I bet he changes his mind once he hears that we could be the ones who catch whoever stole the Dresden Codex though. Let me handle him."

Jesus stifled a smile. "Ok, let me know. Where do you want me today?"

"The usual."

Jesus's morning with the mop bucket went by without incident. The museum was busier than normal because of the news about the missing Dresden Codex, and most of the visitors in front of the replica on display in Merida asked about the tour guides' opinion of the theft. In fact, so many people came to see their replica that Isabella stationed herself outside the display at midmorning so that she could answer people's questions. Jesus was never far away, making sure any footprints were cleaned and smudges wiped from the glass as soon as they appeared.

Isabella didn't say anything when she saw Rodrigo giving one of his unsanctioned tours, instead pretending she didn't see him.

Jesus took his lunch break alone, since his friend was busy with the stream of visitors. He was sitting down on the curb outside, staring off into the distance and thinking about Isabella's upcoming conversation with Santi, when he saw movement out of the corner of his eye. Turning, he saw Balam take a seat on the concrete next to him.

"Still working on getting overseas so I can get to the other codices," Jesus reported. "I made it seem like I could help find the thief, so hopefully they send me to Madrid with Isabella."

"Good. You haven't told anyone about the one under your bed, have you?"

"No, of course not," Jesus said, hurt.

Balam nodded. "And what if your cousin finds it? You don't think he'll do anything, do you?"

"Not without asking me first. I never touch his box of magic—"

"But he's not you."

"He won't do anything," Jesus repeated in a sterner tone.

Balam didn't press the issue.

"Did you just come to ask about Abilio? Why not just stake out the house, distract him when he gets near the bed?"

"For one, nobody's home. He's with your mother at the fruit stand."

"And . . ."

"And two, I just thought about that when I got here. I really came because I have an idea."

"Go on."

"Well, if and when you get to Madrid and steal the codex, what's going to happen?"

"I imagine I'll have to figure out a way to escape," Jesus said after some thought. "Maybe I'll do the same thing—go to the bathroom as soon as I take it, then get away from there."

"They might lock down the whole building. Security will be tighter than in Dresden."

"How do you know? Have you seen it?"

"No—"

"Wait, can you travel that far from the Yucatán?"

"I can see it from the shadow realm, but I'm not strong enough to have a physical form over there. I have to take this one with me."

"You're planning on coming to Madrid too?"

"Of course."

"How am I going to explain that to Isabella? 'No, this is just my cat, he travels everywhere with me.'"

"You just get me to the airport—I'll worry about getting onto the plane."

Jesus shook his head then shrugged. "If you say so."

"Back to the codex. Security will be tighter than at Dresden."

"Again, how do you know."

Balam turned his yellow cat eyes towards Jesus. "One of four existing copies of Mayan writing disappeared. You don't think the remaining examples will be locked down tighter than before?"

Jesus looked off into the distance again and nodded. "That's a good point. What do you have in mind?"

"Get a replica and swap them. There will be a quick moment where neither will be in the case, but everyone there will perceive it as the blink of an eye."

Mentioning Jesus's ability put a hefty dose of impostor

syndrome into his gut. He hadn't thought much about how he would take the document. What had he planned on doing, punching himself in the nose until he bled and hoping for the best? Now, Balam was talking about a full-fledged switch, implying Jesus had some mastery over his ability and wasn't fumbling around in the dark.

"I don't know if I can do this," Jesus said. He brought his knees to his chest and hugged them, feeling deflated.

"Do what?"

"Steal the codex!" Jesus snapped. Then, realizing how loud he had spoken, he looked around, wondering if anyone heard. Or saw him talking to a cat. He exhaled when he confirmed that they were alone.

"I'll be there to help you. But, if it makes you feel better, we can practice now."

Balam ran forward to a discarded orange soda can with a dent in the side sitting on a patch of dirt next to the pavement. "Look at this, and really focus on it. Notice the color, the size, and shape. Nothing else in the world matters but this can . . ."

Balam's voice sounded like it came from right next to Jesus. After shaking off his initial confusion, Jesus looked at the can.

"How do I get into the shadow realm? Do I have to bleed?" Jesus yelled at the cat in the distance.

"You don't have to speak so loud. I can still hear you if you talk normally. And no, not with the power in the land here. Just focus."

"What's going to happen when I'm far from the Yucatán? Like, say, in Madrid?"

"You should also be fine without blood in the presence of the codex, now that you know what's possible. Once you learn how to do it, the teleportation only requires your focus. Now pay attention!"

Jesus stared at the can, ignoring everything else in the world.

It was like he could hear the aluminum and taste the orange color, all of the object's physical characteristics crossing the typical barriers between his senses. He understood and appreciated the can in its totality.

"Now, imagine your shadow is next to the can. Watch yourself pick it up and place it next to your physical body."

Jesus did as he was told but nothing happened.

"Stick with it . . ." Balam urged.

All of a sudden, the can disappeared. Jesus looked down, and it was sitting right next to him. His eyes got wide as he looked at Balam with an open mouth.

"Not bad, right?" Balam said, still far away but sounding right next to him. The cat looked around, found another crushed can—Coca-Cola, this time—and scurried over to it.

"Now, do the same thing. Focus on the object you want, and release the one you don't. Imagine your shadow switching—"

All of a sudden, the can next to Balam changed both color and shape. It became orange and the dent was different. The Coca-Cola can sat next to Jesus on the curb.

"That was fast," Balam said, striding over to Jesus with the pride so typical in solitary cats.

"And you think I can do this in Madrid? The weight doesn't matter?"

"No question. Probably won't be so fast, but if you're patient and keep your eyes on it, you'll be fine."

"Now where can I get a replica," Jesus said, pulling out his phone. "If we're going soon, I can have it shipped to the hotel in Madrid." There weren't many available options, and all of them cost hundreds of dollars. "I can't afford any of these!" Jesus said, defeated.

"Finding the money for one might be easier than escaping when they realize the artifact's been stolen," Balam observed.

"What if . . ." Jesus lowered his voice even more. "What if I take the replica we have here and swap it out?"

"You could, but there's a greater chance people will find out about the swap if the pictures don't align—they're not the same codex. A momentary disappearance replaced by the same object could be a blink; replacement with a different object would stir up feelings of unease and suspicion." Balam thought for a moment. "Could you borrow the money from anyone?"

Jesus thought about the people he knew and could ask for money—none of them had the amount needed for the replica. "I have to see the object to teleport it?" Jesus asked Balam.

"Strictly speaking, no, but without a line of sight you risk teleporting the wrong object."

Jesus nodded. "Why couldn't I try teleporting the codex from here then?"

Balam laughed. "You're much too far. Proximity matters."

"So the magic works better when I'm close?" Jesus sighed and shook his head. "I can't believe I'm going to do this to her, but I don't have any other choice," he said before standing up and going back to work, leaving Balam outside.

Back in Isabella's office at the end of the day, Jesus listened as Isabella informed him that Santi had agreed with their plan. "He said it's worth it if we catch the thief," she explained. "But, I won't be going to Paris after Madrid, so we'll come back here. It's just not in the budget." She seemed sad for a moment, before she got caught up in the thrill of the hunt again. "I assume we'll get there early and watch everyone that walks in . . ."

Her voice faded out as Jesus concentrated on her purse. Then, he pictured a thin piece of plastic with her name on it, sixteen raised numbers, and an expiration date. He imagined his shadow opening her purse and pulling the credit card out from her wallet, then coming over to his physical form and putting it into his pocket.

"Does that sound like a plan to you?"

Startled, Jesus looked at Isabella and blinked twice. "Sorry, I was thinking about the people I saw in Dresden," Jesus said. His dedication to the case elicited a smile from his boss.

"No problem," Isabella said. "I was saying that I can pick you up tomorrow morning and we'll go to the airport. Sound like a plan?"

His hand hidden by the desk between them, Jesus felt his pocket and found a thin piece of hard plastic.

CHAPTER NINE

JESUS AND ISABELLA arrived at the Madrid hotel and waited in a short line at the front desk. They stood in silence, all of their conversation topics long since spent during the flights. Balam still hadn't shown up, and Jesus wondered if the cat got caught on the flight or lost during the layover.

"Can I help who's next?" said the receptionist in Spanish, a young man wearing a slim navy-blue suit. He was tall and lean, with slicked-back hair and a matching permanent smile.

Isabella stepped forward in front of Jesus, taking charge. "We're here to check in," she replied in their shared language.

For the second time, Jesus felt grateful he was in a country where he understood everyone; the first time was in the taxi, trying to get to the correct hotel in the first place.

The receptionist raised his eyebrows, his curiosity piqued. "Where are you from?" he asked with a disarming head tilt.

"Mexico," Isabella said with pride.

"Ah. Welcome to Spain," the receptionist said. After receiving Isabella's printed documentation—Jesus laughed at the folded pieces of paper, to himself, because they both had smartphones—and her identification, he started typing on the computer sitting in front of him on the counter.

"Two rooms." More keys clicked. "And can I see your identification?" he said to Jesus.

Jesus handed over his driver's license, and the receptionist entered more data into his system. "And Mr. Chan, it looks like we have a package for you." The receptionist stepped away and walked around the wall behind his station.

Jesus felt his breath catch in his throat: it was the Madrid Codex replica, bought with Isabella's stolen credit card. He had returned her card that morning, in her car when she picked him up from his house, saying he found the card on the car's floor and joking that she "might need this." He'd thought he could sneak down while she was in her room and get the package, but the thorough receptionist now put him in a vulnerable situation.

The well-dressed hotel worker returned with a box the size of a vinyl record, carrying it with his arms outstretched and leaning back a bit, with the side of the box closest to him digging into his waist. Using a rapid, more aggressive lean in front of his computer, he placed the box on the counter in front of Jesus. "We signed for it, of course."

"Thank you," Jesus said.

"What did you order?" Isabella asked.

"A jacket," Jesus said, thinking on his feet. "It was cold in Germany, and I thought I might need one here too." He thought about the jacket he'd brought from Mexico in his suitcase. It wasn't new by any stretch of the imagination, but Isabella hadn't seen it, so he could pretend the aged look was deliberate.

The receptionist eyed the heavy box with suspicion before his well-practiced smile returned. "Not a bad idea, it's definitely colder here than where you're from!"

Isabella's laugh was too hearty for the joke. As she leaned on the counter with her elbow, Jesus realized she fancied the young man in front of them.

"All right, you guys are good to go," the receptionist said, returning Isabella's gaze. He handed over the two key cards for their adjacent rooms and all of the documents he had taken from them. "Enjoy your stay!"

Jesus put his identification into his pocket and grabbed the box from the counter, making sure he acted like it was as light as a jacket. He braced the muscles in his stomach as he slung the box under one arm and walked with Isabella to the elevator. She didn't pay him any attention, and when he got onto the elevator he switched the box to the same posture with which the receptionist had held it.

Isabella paused before going into her room. "Let's meet tomorrow morning at nine thirty," she said. "Then we'll head over to the Museo de Americá."

Jesus agreed, and they parted ways.

The next morning, Jesus put the Madrid Codex replica into his backpack before putting on his jacket and leaving the room five minutes before the designated time. He sat down in the lobby and watched the people going in and out of the hotel, wondering what their lives were like and where they came from. Most spoke Spanish, like him, but he thought he heard some French, Portuguese, and a Scandinavian language he couldn't place.

Isabella walked out of the elevator wearing tight black pants and black boots, a white shirt, and an olive-green bomber jacket, with a small tan purse slung over her shoulder. In short, she looked like a woman ready for action, like in the movies. Her gaze traveled to the front desk, and she seemed disappointed that the receptionist was a young woman instead of the hotel worker who'd helped them the night before. Then, she spotted Jesus and made her way over to him.

"Ready?" she asked as Jesus stood up.

"Let's go."

After a quick taxi ride, the pair arrived at the towering museum and walked through a pair of columns into the expansive entrance hall.

Isabella wasted no time. "Excuse me," she said, approaching a museum worker.

The older man, wearing a red jacket, turned in her direction with his hands folded in front of him. "How can I help you?" he said.

"We're looking for the Mayan area of the museum. Could you tell us where it is?"

"Of course," the worker said. He stepped back and raised an open hand. "Continue along this hall, go up the stairs, and walk straight forward. You'll see it in a room on the right—you can't miss it."

After thanking him, Isabella led the way. They didn't stop and look at any of the other exhibits. He couldn't explain it, but Jesus got the sense that Isabella saw the museum as a competitor, and that she didn't want the way they organized their collection influencing her own methods. They took one wrong turn, ending up in a room about the Incan Empire, before going into the correct room, where they found the Madrid Codex front and center.

The Mayan script was unfolded and squeezed between two thick pieces of glass, the entire document spanning a dozen paces. Both Jesus and Isabella took a moment standing still at a distance, then they both approached the pages and inspected the symbols. Isabella emerged from her reverie first.

"You haven't recognized anyone yet, have you?" she whispered, standing next to him but not looking at him.

Jesus remembered that they were the good guys, staking out a valuable artifact and looking for the thieves. Or so she thought.

In fact, he was the one coming to steal the codex. He knew Isabella would be consumed by guilt if she ever found out, but that a tiny part of her would delight in her proximity to the heist.

He didn't tell her that he hadn't paid attention to anyone on their walk to the room. He looked at the faces in the room with him—there weren't many, since the museum had been open for less than an hour—and reported that he didn't recognize anyone. There weren't any men with white hair, but he did see a black cat hiding behind a display in the corner.

Balam couldn't communicate with him while Isabella was around; he was on his own.

"Keep looking. We'll stay here all day if we have to," she said, setting her jaw.

Remembering Balam's instructions, Jesus started concentrating on the codex in front of him. The glyphs came to life, wiggling and moving, and the edges of the pages started glowing as they took over his awareness. In the back of his mind, he realized there was an added step he hadn't practiced—the codex, as displayed, was unfolded, so his shadow form would have to both fold the real codex and unfold the replica in his backpack for a successful switch of the objects.

"Did you know this was a replica?" Isabella asked, disrupting Jesus's concentration.

At hearing the word "replica," his stomach dropped to his feet. He shook his head, clearing his thoughts. "What?" he asked, turning towards her and breaking his gaze. When he looked back at the Mayan writing, it looked the same as it did when he had first walked into the room.

"This one is a replica. It says the original is here in the museum though," Isabella explained, reading the placard on the right side of the display. Then, her eyes opened and her head shot back. "Whoever comes to steal it won't be here . . . They'll go for the real thing!"

She hurried back to the hallway that led into the room. Realizing that Jesus wasn't following her, she came back and grabbed his arm. "We're looking for the thief in the wrong place!"

Isabella led Jesus back towards the entrance, looking for museum staff the entire time. She found someone at the front desk. "Excuse me, we're from the Great Museum of the Mayan World in Merida, here to see the Madrid Codex."

"Ok, well the exhibit is up—" the woman at the desk said.

Isabella cut her off. "No, the real Madrid Codex." She looked like she wanted to say something else—something about the potential theft of the document, Jesus thought—but decided against it.

"Let me call the curator." The woman working the front desk picked up a phone receiver and pressed a button. Then, she turned away and cupped a hand around the mouthpiece, speaking at a low volume.

Isabella, impatient, looked around at the visitors streaming into the museum and told Jesus he should be keeping an eye out too. Jesus turned around and scanned the faces of the new arrivals, making a show of focus for his boss.

"Miss?" the front desk woman said.

Isabella and Jesus both turned around.

"The curator is coming out now."

Isabella and Jesus took a seat with a view of everyone walking in. "Just in case," Isabella said, in the event that the thief had decided that walking in through the front door was part of their plan.

The curator appeared after the pair were waiting for almost half an hour. He was a tiny bald man, with age spots on his hands and small square glasses perched at the end of his nose.

The woman at the front desk pointed out Isabella and Jesus to him, and he walked over to their position with slow steps.

"Hello, my name is Dr. Fernandez. Welcome to the museum." His words were slow and deliberate, like he spent most of his time with relics instead of humans.

"I'm Isabella Canche, and this is Jesus Chan. We're from the Great Museum of the Mayan World in Merida, Mexico—I'm the curator there."

"Always a pleasure to meet a fellow colleague. I must say, most museum experts aren't as beautiful as you."

Jesus knew Isabella's disdain for the focus on her physical appearance, but instead of a grimace, she smiled.

"Why, thank you," she said, fluttering her eyelashes.

"I've been told you're interested in seeing the Madrid Codex . . ." Dr. Fernandez said.

"Yes, very much."

"You know, we typically prefer fellow museums call us so we can schedule these things." As Dr. Fernandez said this, he tilted his head down and looked over his glasses at Isabella.

Isabella turned on the charm. "I know, I know. I wouldn't appreciate it if someone did this to me." She put a hand on his shoulder. "Makes it that much more meaningful that you took the time to see us at all."

"You heard about the theft in Dresden? Such a shame," the curator said, before flashing Isabella a smile. "Come on, let's go take a look."

They walked at the curator's slow pace into the depths of the museum, and Jesus thought that the old man might've left his office at the first call from the front desk, that it took him almost half an hour to make it to the entrance.

"It's amazing—we don't have anyone here to see the codex for weeks, and now there's been two in one day!" the old curator said.

Jesus heard Isabella take in a quick breath. "Wait, someone else came to see it?" she said. She looked at Jesus with wide eyes.

"A student, here from . . . I forget which country, but they didn't speak Spanish very well. Took me forever to understand what they wanted!" the curator said with a laugh.

Isabella suffered for the rest of the slow walk. When they made it to the climate-controlled room where the real Madrid Codex lived, she almost burst in and tackled the young man inspecting the spread-open document beneath the glass. The student looked at the new arrivals with curiosity, and Jesus thought he looked like a younger version of the curator. Isabella elbowed him and looked at him with imploring eyes, and Jesus shook his head, indicating that he hadn't seen the man before.

"They also want to see the Madrid Codex," the curator explained, in Spanish. "They came from Mexico!"

The student's eyes didn't register anything until he heard "Mexico," then he walked forward and introduced himself as Noah, from the Netherlands. Noah, Dr. Fernandez, and Isabella struggled through a conversation about their respective careers, with plenty of help from translations via Noah's phone, and none of them noticed Jesus staring at the Madrid Codex.

The replica on display and the real codex both came alive for him in the same way, but the real codex had an additional magnetic pull that Jesus couldn't deny. A surge of energy, the author calling out to him from beyond the grave. Jesus stared at the document, imagining a shadow form of himself folding the document, carrying it to his backpack, swapping it with the replica he'd ordered, and putting the unfolded replica back where the real one was before.

He stared and stared, tied to the existence of the ancient document while playing another film inside his mind, one in the shadow realm that he hoped occurred in his physical space. Then, a blink . . .

"Jesus, what do you think about the codex?" Dr. Fernandez asked.

"He's full Maya, so this was written by his ancestors," Isabella added with pride.

Jesus readjusted his backpack, noticing the reduced weight. He reached back and felt the bottom, discovering the same shape as the replica. He'd done it. The Madrid Codex on the table in front of him seemed a bit newer, but not enough to cause suspicion.

"I think it looks old," he said.

Everyone laughed, including Noah, who didn't need his phone for the translation.

Isabella and Jesus spent the next hour with the curator and the student, looking at the various symbols while the curator explained what they meant. After Isabella brought up the Dresden Codex again, the old man also went over the extensive security measures they'd added since the theft. They were so effective, in fact, that even a black cat couldn't get into the space without the curator's stamp of approval—Balam never made an appearance.

Meanwhile, Jesus was racked by nerves and felt like he was sweating more in the climate-controlled room than he ever had in the Mexican sun. He marveled at how accurate the replica was—even the curator couldn't tell the swap had occurred—and chalked the oversight up to the man being distracted by visitors.

When the curator said he had a meeting, a veiled dismissal of the trio, they all left, to Jesus's great relief. Right outside the door, Isabella pulled Jesus to the side.

"You didn't see the student in Dresden?" she said, not giving up on the chase for the thief.

"No, I never saw him before."

"Well, the codex looks safe enough, inside the room," she said, leading the way down the aisle and away from the curator's realm. "But we should still stay around the museum, just in case."

They were almost to the museum's main area when Jesus heard the curator yelling behind them. "Hey! You! Stop!"

Startled, Jesus rushed forward and pushed the double doors, leaving Isabella behind. He turned around and saw the curator shuffling down the hall towards them with a business card in hand.

"This number goes directly to my office. Give me a call if you have any more questions!"

Both the curator and Isabella stared at Jesus. All he could come up with was that he really had to find the bathroom.

CHAPTER TEN

Jesus and Isabella were walking out of the museum when they ran into Hugh and one of the men he had been with in Dresden. The twins stopped a few paces from each other when they saw the other version of themselves, Jesus under the columns at the museum entrance and Hugh on the concrete sidewalk.

"What are you doing here?" Hugh said to Jesus as the four people approached each other. His words sounded like an attack.

"We came to see the Madrid Codex," Jesus replied, his voice level.

"I thought you went back to Merida," Hugh said.

"I did. And then we came to Madrid. You remember Isabella, right?"

Hugh transformed into a charming gentleman. "Of course, how could I forget." He took her hand and shook it before leaning in for an air kiss on the cheek.

A blushing Isabella seemed taken by surprise at the show of familiarity.

"So you went back to Mexico then flew back out to Spain?"

Jesus nodded.

"Wow, you've never crossed the Atlantic, then do so twice in a few weeks! Looks like you're finally out seeing the world. I'm impressed with you, brother."

"I ran into Hugh in Dresden," Jesus explained to Isabella. "He was at the presentation too. How long were you trapped in the room again?" He could guess how mad his brother had been at the inconvenience.

"The entire day. The police wouldn't let us leave without a thorough interview, all recorded on video."

"It was terrible," Hugh's friend added, in French-accented Spanish.

"Oh right, you remember Dennis? He was there too," Hugh said. "Dennis, this is my twin, Jesus, and his boss, Isabella." There was an almost imperceivable stress on the word "boss." He looked at Isabella. "Dennis works at the Musée de l'Homme, the anthropology museum in Paris."

"Mucho gusto," Isabella and Dennis both said, shaking hands.

Jesus nodded at Hugh's friend and didn't extend an arm. "What are you two doing here?" he asked Hugh.

"Same thing you're doing: seeing the Madrid Codex."

Jesus saw Isabella readjust her stance out of the corner of his eye. She gave the pair a sweet smile. "We already saw it, but we can see it again," she said before turning towards Jesus and widening her eyes a bit, urging his cooperation.

Jesus's voice caught in his throat. With a stolen codex in his backpack, the last place he wanted to go was back inside the museum.

"We wouldn't want to derail your plans," Hugh said, searching for a polite exit.

"No, we don't have any plans! We'd love to come with you," Isabella insisted.

"Let's go then!" Dennis said with enthusiasm and a flirtatious grin directed at Isabella.

While they walked, Hugh explained that the pair had gone from Dresden to Madrid, and that they were heading to Paris next. "Seeing all three codices in the same trip. I couldn't imagine going back to Mexico City just to fly back out again," Hugh said. He looked at Jesus. "Are you getting tired of airplanes yet?"

Jesus, racked with paranoia about the ancient relic in his backpack, mumbled that he didn't mind, that he just slept the entire time.

"Man, I bet you have a great time with this one," Hugh said to Isabella, tilting his head towards Jesus.

Isabella laughed.

They got back into the room that displayed the Madrid Codex replica, and everyone stopped talking in reverence to the ancient object. Isabella grabbed Jesus's arm and held him back while Hugh and Dennis got a closer look.

"They were in Dresden too?" she hissed. She looked like she was about to say something, thought for a moment, then said, "Dennis could have stolen the Dresden Codex!"

"Or Hugh," Jesus added.

"I'm not saying that," Isabella said, holding up her hands. "He's your brother."

"But still, it's possible."

Isabella watched the pair inspecting the glyphs on the aged document. "They were interviewed by the police, but maybe they hid it inside the room, then came back and retrieved it . . ." she said.

"Maybe," Jesus said, glad she didn't suspect him whatsoever.

Hugh got to the placard that provided details about the display. "This is only a replica," he said to Dennis. He turned to Isabella. "Did you know that?"

Isabella froze, thinking of ways she could keep the pair far from the real codex.

Jesus didn't think twice about telling the truth. "We know; we met with the curator and saw the real thing," he said, rubbing the privileged access in his twin's face.

Hugh looked at Jesus like his twin had said he preferred drinking his eggs raw—a mixture of confusion and disgust. "And you weren't going to say anything?"

"It looks the same as this," Jesus replied.

"I want to see the real thing," Dennis said. "Do you think we could talk to the curator and see it too?"

Before Isabella could mention that they had the curator's direct number, Jesus said they could go to the front desk and ask for a meeting, knowing the curator was busy.

"Let's do it, I don't care about the replica," Hugh said, storming out of the room.

Dennis, Isabella, and Jesus followed him back to the entrance.

"Well, I think we're going to take off," Jesus said, still worried about the potential discovery of the stolen codex.

Isabella said they would wait, and they stood behind Hugh while he demanded an audience with the curator.

"I'm sorry, but he's in a meeting," the front desk woman said. She seemed confused at seeing Isabella and Jesus standing behind Hugh and Dennis but didn't say anything.

"We came from Mexico City and Paris to see the Madrid Codex, not a replica," Hugh said, getting indignant.

The woman at the front desk stood her ground. "Well, I'm sorry, but you'll have to make do with seeing the replica on display," she said. She went to the computer and, after a few clicks, raised her gaze and looked at an angry Hugh again. "And it looks like he's in meetings through the rest of the week. Probably next week too. There's not much we can do for you."

Hugh looked at Isabella and Jesus. "And you two saw it?" he said in disbelief.

"Sure, we were with the curator up until we left and ran into you," Isabella said with a smug confidence Jesus hadn't seen before.

Dennis put a hand on Hugh's shoulder. Hugh twisted his body in anger. Then, he calmed himself and smiled at the woman blocking access to what he wanted.

"Look, is there anything you can do to help us? We'd really appreciate it."

A change went over the woman. Her face relaxed and she tilted her head, as if seeing Hugh for the first time. She started speaking without taking her eyes off of him.

"Well, his current meeting should be done by this afternoon. If you come back around three, you should be able to get back there and see it."

Hugh thanked her in a singsong voice full of sincerity.

Jesus looked at Isabella and felt bad for her; she was stunned about the woman's attitude reversal. He had seen Hugh pull the stunt many times before, most often with teachers and his mother, and knew his twin got his way whenever he kept his temper in check.

"Well then, looks like we have a few hours to kill!" Hugh said, turning to his companion.

Dennis looked at Isabella. "Should we all go get lunch?"

Jesus hoped Isabella would say no, that they had other plans, but he also knew how much stock she placed in him having seen the pair in both Dresden and Madrid. In her eyes, it couldn't be a coincidence.

"We do need to eat," she said, looking at Jesus, who shook his head. Ignoring his disagreement, she told the pair they would join them.

They ended up at a sidewalk cafe a short cab ride from the

museum. Hugh ordered tapas for the table and somehow managed a visit from the manager, who agreed to give them a steep discount because they were, as Hugh said, "Going to recommend the place to everyone at the museum."

Isabella did most of the talking, since it was obvious Dennis was interested in her on a more personal level and Hugh couldn't care less about anything his twin said.

While Jesus half listened, staring at the people passing by, he saw a black cat with too-large yellow eyes slinking along the building. The cat met his gaze but didn't approach. As Jesus watched, a large orange tabby emerged from a nearby alley, stalking what Jesus guessed was Balam. For a moment, it appeared that the orange cat would rush forward and pounce, but before it could move, the black cat turned around and stared.

The orange cat rushed away, fearing for its life.

Jesus thought he saw the black cat shake its head before lifting and licking its paw.

"I think you can't wait for a few days at home," Dennis said at the periphery of Jesus's awareness.

Isabella nudged Jesus when he didn't answer.

Jesus brought his attention back to the table. Dennis repeated the statement, and Jesus realized Dennis's words were directed at him.

"Oh yes, that will be nice."

"He can spend some time with our mother," Hugh said, laughing.

Neither Isabella nor Dennis understood why Hugh thought the statement was funny.

The black cat was gone when Jesus looked again.

Dennis and Hugh made a big show of fighting for the check, and in the end, they agreed that Hugh would pay because

Dennis would be in charge of showing him around Paris at the conclusion of his European trip.

Jesus assumed they would all part ways after lunch. He was wrong.

"Heading back to the museum, right?" Isabella asked as they stood up from the table.

"To see the real Madrid Codex, yes," Dennis responded.

"Are you guys going to see the city? Maybe we can all meet up later," Hugh said. Jesus knew his twin well enough that he knew his brother had no intention of making that happen.

"No, I think we're going with you back to the museum. I want to see it again—there's just so much history, you know?" Isabella said, flashing a sweet smile to Dennis. She had no intention of letting the pair near the codex without her watchful gaze on them.

"Great!" Dennis said. "I'll take care of the cab."

Hugh objected, saying he would take care of the cab himself, but Dennis wouldn't have it.

Jesus was about to say he wasn't feeling well, that he was going back to the hotel, when the cab screeched to a stop in front of them. They rode back to the museum, and Dennis paid the driver.

"Shall we?" Dennis said, holding a bent arm up in Isabella's direction.

Isabella coiled her arm around his, and they started walking towards the entrance.

"I'll just sit outside," Jesus said. "I want to watch the people."

Isabella turned around and nodded, knowing Jesus's intentions right away. Hugh looked at him like he was crazy and scoffed at his twin while shaking his head. "Suit yourself," he said before following the pair inside.

Jesus wasn't alone long before the same black cat slunk over to where he sat on a bench with a clear view of the entrance.

"I didn't realize you'd be with the woman all the time," Balam said, sitting down and watching the entrance with Jesus.

Jesus looked around, making sure nobody was nearby. "The only way I could get over here was with her."

"And your twin's here too. Quite the reunion," Balam observed. "He's powerful."

"I know."

"Do you?" Balam said.

Something about the way the cat asked the question made Jesus pause. "I guess I never really thought about it. He just always gets his way, no matter what."

"That's his power—the gift of tongues. Your ancestor used to call them snakes."

A lifetime of watching Hugh work his magic flashed through Jesus's memory, and he realized the answer had been right in front of him the whole time. "He's been using his power forever. Why could he use his and I couldn't use mine?"

Balam chuckled. "Under what stars would you have learned that you could teleport objects? For Hugh, I'm sure it was only a matter of time until he learned that if he said things just the right way, he could get whatever he wanted."

The transformation of the woman at the front desk made more sense in light of the new information. "Does it work with languages too?" Jesus asked, thinking about how his brother had no problem learning Spanish after they grew up speaking Mayan, and how he spoke English as well as anyone in Mexico.

"Especially with languages. The priests with the gift of tongues were responsible for preaching to the masses far and wide."

Balam and Jesus sat in silence while they watched an overworked female teacher herd a group of children from a bus into the museum.

"All that practice explains why his shadow is fully formed. It's strong, and almost ten feet tall—taller than most of the twelve priests'."

Even though Jesus was used to his twin overshadowing him, the mention of Hugh's more robust alternate form was like a spear in his gut. The shadow realm and magic were supposed to be his thing, learned about and developed far from—and without—his twin. All he could utter was one word: "How?"

"You're a twin. You've heard of the hero twins of the Maya?"

Jesus nodded. "Hugh's real name is Hunahpu."

Balam stretched, arching his back while his front legs were extended, his tail straight up in the air.

"Does his name give him more power?" Jesus asked.

"Doesn't hurt," Balam replied. "Twins can get more powerful than normal humans. It's easier for them to learn magic, and their shadow form grows strong with very little practice. They were almost always brought into the priesthood, so that they wouldn't grow stronger than the priests and take control."

"So, Hugh's shadow is already much stronger than mine. Let's add it to the list of things he's better at," Jesus said, hanging his head.

"Yours is already looking healthier—still the same size, but no longer frail. Wasn't it easier to get the second codex? That's because you're more powerful!"

"Well, I didn't have to bleed. How'd you know I have it?"

"The power trails behind you like the smell of cooked onions." Balam turned his yellow eyes towards Jesus. "You'll catch up to your twin soon enough, once the codices are back in the Yucatán. Now you just have to get this one back home."

CHAPTER ELEVEN

THE NEXT MORNING, Jesus found himself facing a difficult decision after Isabella messaged him saying that they were returning to the museum. After rolling his eyes, he panicked: Should he keep the stolen codex with him in his backpack, or leave it behind in the hotel? He paced in front of his bed, with the backpack containing the Madrid Codex sitting on a tangle of blankets.

Either let it out of his sight, or risk taking the stolen property back to the museum. Again.

Someone knocked on his door.

"One second!" Jesus yelled.

"Take your time," Isabella said from the hall.

Jesus bobbed his head and rubbed his hands together while he thought. Then, he rushed forward and put the backpack into his suitcase before zipping it shut. He thought about putting it into the closet but decided it didn't matter. Then, he grabbed his wallet and his phone and opened the door.

Isabella stood up from where she leaned on the wall. "Good morning," she said. She had a similar outfit on as the day before —the same black pants and boots—but this time, she wore a maroon shirt beneath her olive jacket. She started towards the elevator.

"I figure we can go hang around the museum, see if anyone else from Dresden shows up."

"Did Dennis or Hugh say they'd be coming back?" Jesus asked. After Isabella's second trip to see the codex, the group had come back out and said a few brief goodbyes before going their separate ways.

"Dennis said they're going to another museum today," Isabella reported. "He was messaging me all night, trying to get me to go out for drinks with them."

"And you didn't feel like it?"

Isabella turned and looked at Jesus with mock seriousness, her eyebrows furrowed at his question. "I was tired," she said with a shrug.

They rode the elevator down to the lobby then hailed a cab outside the hotel.

"So, what's the plan for today? Sit around and look at the people going into the museum?" Jesus said without any effort at hiding his disappointment.

"More or less, yes. It's the main reason Santi got on board with sending you with me. We have to see if the thief shows up."

"I was thinking about that," Jesus said. "Stealing the Dresden Codex was a major risk, and probably required a lot of preparation. What are the chances the same person tries to steal this codex in the few days we are here?"

"Well, what if they're scouting the area?"

"Like Hugh and Dennis could've been doing yesterday?" Jesus said.

Isabella said, "Them, or others. But I really don't think they had anything to do with it. Women's intuition," she said, tapping her stomach.

"Still, this kind of luck is the kind of thing you see in movies. Seems like there's little chance of the thief showing up."

"We have to try," Isabella said with finality.

Jesus didn't press the issue.

The pair got dropped off at the museum entrance soon after it opened. Jesus saw a black cat sneaking around nearby but didn't watch him for too long so that Isabella wouldn't notice him as well. They spent the morning seated on a bench in front of the building, then checked out the display again when Isabella said she "wanted to make sure the man from Germany with the white hair didn't get in another way."

It was almost lunchtime before Isabella's resolve showed signs of cracking. "They could be eating somewhere around here, scouting out escape routes . . ." she said, scanning the museum's entrance from her spot on the bench.

"Maybe we could go eat lunch close by—I'll keep an eye out and see if I recognize anyone."

Isabella sighed and hung her head.

"What's wrong?" Jesus said.

"I gave up a trip to Paris so you could come and try finding the thief. But the more I think about it, the more you might be right: Why wouldn't the thief take a good long time before stealing the second codex? Let the heat die down, you know?"

Jesus leaned forward, resting his elbows on his knees. He lowered his head so he could look Isabella in the eye. "I'm sorry you didn't get to go to Paris."

"Me too," she said.

"Maybe we can enjoy our time in Madrid a bit more to make up for it, instead of sitting at the museum? We don't leave until tomorrow night; we still have the rest of the day and tomorrow morning." Jesus felt a pang of guilt that he'd manipulated Isabella in Merida with promises of catching a thief, and he wondered if Hugh ever felt the same way when he talked his way into getting what he wanted.

Isabella looked at Jesus, smiled, and shook her head. "So you got a trip to Madrid for nothing," she said, joking.

"Look at it this way: if we're supposed to run into them, we will. Whether it's here, or somewhere nearby."

"You sound like you're a religious man all of a sudden," Isabella said.

"Sometimes it pays to believe in something greater than yourself."

Isabella nodded, and Jesus took the lead. He hailed a cab and directed the driver to the tourist area, without specifying what he meant. The driver took them to the Puerta del Sol, and from there the pair walked around, visiting as many of the major tourist attractions as they could.

Every so often, Jesus would see a black cat, always across the street or off in the distance.

They returned to the hotel that night, and Jesus found the suitcase, backpack, and codex right where he left them. Balam was curled on the pillow. The shadow jaguar reported that he had spent the day watching the Madrid Codex; he had made sure the cleaning lady didn't investigate. Jesus realized that the black cats he saw around Madrid weren't Balam—he had a feeling that he'd find black cats slinking around in any major city if he looked for them.

The next morning Isabella asked if they could visit the Estadio Santiago Bernabéu, Real Madrid's home stadium. "My dad was a fan, and he always wanted to go there."

With the Madrid Codex left in the hotel room under Balam's watchful gaze, Jesus and Isabella took a tour of the stadium before taking a cab to Madrid's Centro. There, they enjoyed their remaining time in Spain before returning to the hotel and preparing for their departure.

Jesus faced the same challenge he had in Dresden: What should he do with the codex on the flight back to Merida? Balam had disappeared, so he couldn't ask for guidance. Thinking about what would happen if the airline lost his luggage, he decided it would stay with him, just like on his first flight back home. Except now, he had to think about Isabella—she would see what he had in his backpack if security decided his bag required a thorough search again. And there was no way he could claim he'd bought a replica this time, since she had been with him the entire time he was in Madrid.

Somehow, he'd have to go through security at a separate time.

Isabella was waiting for him when he got to the hotel lobby. "Ready?" he asked.

She nodded, and he could tell something was on her mind.

"Still thinking about the thief?"

"More about how stupid I was to think they would be here so soon."

"Hey, it was worth a try," Jesus said. "We could've been the heroes."

Isabella looked at Jesus with sad eyes and a forced smile. "I think we both watch too many movies."

The pair left the hotel, and Jesus still didn't see Balam anywhere. He searched for him outside the airport as well and never found him. Part of him was worried, but another part remembered that if the shadow jaguar had existed for hundreds of years without issue, he could figure out a way to get back to Merida. For all Jesus knew, the cat could be slinking around the tarmac now, on his way to the plane.

They checked their bags and started towards the security line. Jesus put his plan into action. "Hey, I've got to go to the bathroom," he said, gesturing towards the restroom outside of the security checkpoint.

"Ok," Isabella said, moving towards the wall.

Jesus feigned embarrassment. "It's going to be a while," he said, clutching his stomach.

Isabella nodded. "That's all right, take your time." She pulled out her phone and leaned against the wall.

Jesus went into the bathroom and found an empty stall. He didn't have to go, but he figured he might as well wait her out. If she got nervous she might miss the flight, she'd go on without him.

After almost half an hour playing on his phone, he heard Isabella's voice from the entrance. "Jesus, is everything all right in there?"

Being in Spain, everyone spoke Spanish, so Jesus assumed most of the men in the bathroom understood what she said. His ears burned. "Fine, it's just taking a while," he yelled.

"Well, try and hurry," she said.

He stayed on his phone until a rustling from the other men in the bathroom got his attention.

"Jesus?" Isabella said from inside the bathroom. "Come on, we have to go. We can find another bathroom on the other side of security."

Jesus couldn't maintain the deception. When he stood up, he found that one of his legs was asleep. He opened the door and came face-to-face with Isabella.

"Sorry about that," he said, embarrassed. A pair of men at the urinals snickered before turning their gaze away from him.

"I'll wait outside," Isabella said, every shred of patience gone.

Jesus washed his hands and met Isabella outside, still searching for a separate way through security, one where Isabella wouldn't see what he carried in his backpack.

They waited in the security line together, and Isabella had her identification and boarding pass scanned first. Jesus approached the guard as she went to the closest line for the metal detector. He got waved through, then made his way towards the metal detector line farthest from his boss.

Isabella looked at him, the question obvious in her gaze.

"This one looks like it'll be faster!" Jesus said, hurrying away so she wouldn't accompany him.

It wasn't faster. In fact, it was quite a bit slower. As Jesus watched in horror, Isabella got through her line and grabbed her things before he even walked through the metal detector. Then, she started walking towards him.

Jesus felt his racing heart and started sorting through the various potential explanations that popped into his mind. Whenever he thought he had a viable option, his nerves shot it down, and so he found himself staring at the conveyor belt while his bag passed though, with Isabella mere steps away.

The female guard, noticing Jesus staring at the screen, smiled and said, "Your flight's about to leave?"

Jesus, caught off guard, replied, "Huh?"

"You look nervous. Is your flight about to leave?" the guard repeated.

"That, and his stomach's bothering him," Isabella chimed in.

"That's the worst," the guard said. When Jesus's backpack appeared from the back of the X-ray machine, she grabbed the bin and slid it farther along.

"Don't miss it!" the guard said, turning her attention back to the screen.

Isabella picked up Jesus's backpack. "What do you have in here? Doesn't feel like anything at all!"

Jesus still couldn't explain why both codices seemed much lighter when they were carried, but he was curious that the phenomenon also happened to Isabella. "Something to read," he managed, grabbing the bag from her and slinging it over his shoulders.

He forgot to go back to the bathroom on the way to their gate. After Isabella reminded him, he went in for a few minutes and came back out, reporting that he felt much better. They had boarded the plane and were on the tarmac when Isabella asked about Hugh.

"Do you and Hugh not talk very much?" she said.

Jesus put his head back against the seat. "Not really. We're very different people."

"I can see that. About as different as twins can get. You didn't even know he was going to be in Madrid."

"Imagine my surprise when I ran into him in Dresden. My host said there were other Mexicans there, and guess who it was?"

"Hugh," Isabella replied. "You two didn't even talk much when we were all together. Have you always been like this?"

Jesus sighed. "No, not always."

"What happened?"

When Jesus paused, Isabella put her hands up and shook her head. "None of my business. I'm sorry."

"No, it's fine." Jesus gathered his thoughts, putting the pieces together for himself as well as for her. He remembered months of drifting apart, but it had all culminated in one final rupture. "In essence, Hugh was upset my mother stayed in Merida when we were growing up. As he sees it, going to a larger city, Mexico City in this case, provides greater opportunities."

Isabella waited with her hands folded in her lap.

"Well, right as he was about to leave for school in Mexico City, the two of them got into it. They were both yelling, but she decided she was done. She told him she was going to church to pray for him, that she loved him very much, and she would see him soon.

"Hugh wasn't done. He asked her why she still had a bunch

of Mayan statues and trinkets if she believed in God—I think he was mad that she still had a tie to Merida and the Mayan culture there. She grabbed her Bible and walked out. Hugh lit a fire and burned everything Mayan she owned, including some books she owned about the Mayan creation myths. I didn't do anything to stop him."

"The Popol Vuh?" Isabella asked.

"I think she had a copy of that, and the Books of Chilam Balam."

"What did your mother say when she got back?"

"She got back from church late that night; Hugh was already gone. She asked me where her stuff had gone, and I showed her the remains of the fire in the backyard. I've never seen her look so hurt, and I've never felt so ashamed. She went to her room while I swept up the ashes and tried washing away the stains with a bucket of water. The black marks are still there.

"Hugh came back for Christmas that year and acted like the whole thing hadn't happened. We never talked about it, and nothing's been the same since."

CHAPTER TWELVE

"Wake up," Abilio said, turning on the light inside the room he shared with Jesus.

Jesus rolled over and pulled the sheet over his head.

"I said, 'Wake up!'" Abilio reached forward and yanked the sheet, pulling it off of the bed. Jesus, wearing just his underwear, curled into a ball and hugged himself while forcing his face into the pillow.

Abilio bundled the sheet around his arms and tossed it onto the other side of the bed.

Jesus reached behind him, searching for the sheet. When he didn't find it, he lifted his head and squinted at his cousin standing at the foot of their bed.

"What writing do you have to keep safe?" Abilio asked.

Jesus sat straight up while turning so that his feet hung off of the bed. How could Abilio know about the codices? He rubbed his eyes with the heels of his hands, rubbing away the sleep and wondering if he was still dreaming. "What did you say?"

"More like what you said. You kept muttering that you had to keep the writing safe. Sounded pretty desperate if you ask me. What were you dreaming about?"

Jesus still didn't have his bearings. "What time is it?" he asked.

"Three. Doña Beatriz told me to come wake you up. She needs you at the fruit stand this evening, said something about taking dinner to Gloria."

After getting back to Merida that morning, he fell asleep at noon even though he had slept on the plane back from Madrid. And now he was called into action again, just three short hours later.

"Ok, I'm getting up."

"Good. Now what writing were you talking about?"

Jesus thought for a moment. He was still groggy, and stringing together a lie wasn't forthcoming. So, he told the truth. "The Mayan writing. There's only four examples left in the whole world. I've been thinking about it a lot lately, ever since I saw Hugh's presentation about the one in Mexico City. I guess my thoughts spilled over to my dreams."

"Sounded like it was pretty urgent," Abilio said, inspecting his nails. He picked at a cuticle then rubbed it, as if overcoming the habit.

"What did I say?"

"Protect the documents; can't lose the words; save the power —stuff like that. Must've been some dream." Abilio looked at Jesus with suspicious eyes as Jesus got up and hurried to the bathroom.

Jesus brushed his teeth and splashed water on his face. He used the toilet and washed his hands before coming out and finding Abilio sitting on their bed, scrolling through his phone. "Shouldn't you be going back to the fruit stand?" he asked his cousin.

"Beatriz said I could take my time, while it's slow, since we'll be there until late. If she's taking some time on a Saturday, so can I."

Jesus nodded and sorted through his still-packed luggage for clothes. He put on a pair of black jeans and a black AC/DC T-shirt.

"What's under the bed?" Abilio asked, without looking up from his phone.

Jesus felt his stomach drop.

"What do you mean?" he asked, feigning nonchalance.

"You were trying to be sneaky and put something under the bed when you got home this morning."

Jesus furrowed his brow and shook his head, as if Abilio was speaking nonsense.

"When you first got home, before we left for the fruit stand and you took your little nap? Pretend all you want, I saw what I saw."

Abilio continued when Jesus didn't respond.

"I could've looked when you were in the bathroom—the bag's right next to my box of magic supplies, after all. But I figured I could just ask you." Abilio looked at Jesus and smiled. "The look on your face right now was worth the wait."

Jesus sighed while focusing on relaxing the muscles in his face. He looked at Abilio. "If I show you, you have to promise not to tell anyone."

"Of course," Abilio said.

"Say those words: 'I promise not to tell anyone.'"

Abilio rolled his eyes. "I promise not to tell anyone."

Satisfied, Jesus lowered himself onto the floor and reached under the bed for the bag that now held both the Dresden and Madrid codices. It wasn't until he was halfway back to standing that he realized he could have just teleported the bag to him—using his powers for mundane tasks was still a foreign concept.

Jesus laid the bag on the bed. He exhaled, letting the escaping air calm him.

A curious Abilio stood up and put his phone on the bed where he had sat a moment before.

Jesus pulled the zipper, opening one side of the bag. He looked at Abilio. "Keep your mouth shut."

Caught up in the moment, Abilio pinched his lips together.

"I mean about what I'm about to show you," Jesus said, still serious.

"I already promised, just show me what's in the bag!" Abilio yelled.

Jesus opened his backpack all the way and peeled the front back, showing the two ancient documents to Abilio.

"A collection of old papers? Taking your work home from the museum now?" Abilio joked.

"No, these are two of the codices I was talking about!"

"Wait, two of the four that exist in the entire world?"

Jesus nodded.

"How much do they cost?"

"Cost? I don't even know if I could sell them without getting into trouble."

The truth dawned on Abilio. "You stole them? How?"

Jesus explained what had happened in Dresden, how the codex ended up in his backpack when he got a bloody nose, then mentioned meeting Balam in the backyard garden. Abilio, well-versed in Santeria, didn't doubt any of the story for a second. "I knew magic worked!" he said.

"This magic isn't the same as what you're used to," Jesus said, walking out of the bedroom. "There aren't any spells." Talking about Balam reminded him that he hadn't seen the cat since arriving back in Merida. He left the house through the back door and went into the backyard.

Abilio followed him the entire time, talking about his own magic spells. "We cast a spell for more money, and now we have something priceless!" he said, running his fingers through his hair. "The spell was too powerful. Maybe if we take down the total amount, and use a shorter candle, we can get something we can actually sell . . ." He looked at his cousin, watching as Jesus searched where the concrete wall surrounding their backyard met the roof on both sides of their house.

"What are we doing back here?" Abilio said. He looked at the trees laden with fruit. "Wait, we just picked those clean this morning . . ." he observed.

"It's because of the codices," Jesus explained. "The power from them in the house makes the fruit grow like crazy." He went back to the first side of the house he'd inspected. "Balam?" he hissed.

"You're looking for the cat?"

"I guess he's still not back from Madrid."

"You took the cat to Madrid?" Abilio asked, confused.

"He took himself. But I was with Isabella the entire time, so I couldn't make sure he got back on the plane."

"Ok, so the cat came from the shadow realm and told you that if you could somehow bring back all the Mayan codices to Mexico, you could give all of the Maya magical powers?"

"More or less, yes," Jesus said, accepting that Balam wasn't there. He walked back inside, followed by Abilio.

"What kind of magical powers?" Abilio said with a mischievous glint in his eye.

"Well . . ." Jesus said, looking around. His gaze settled on a wooden spoon sitting upright in a ceramic container on the counter. "Sit down," he told Abilio, and the two of them took a seat at the dining room table.

"See that wooden spoon?" Jesus asked.

"Beatriz's favorite," Abilio said, a joke about the stories he'd heard about her favorite punishment tool when the twins were younger. Some mothers preferred the spatula, others the chancla, but Beatriz always found the wooden spoon the most accessible. Abilio hadn't experienced the utensil himself, having come to live with them when he was already older, but the threat still loomed over the house like a loaded mousetrap waiting for a curious rodent.

"Ok, keep your eye on it," Jesus said. He focused on the spoon, then imagined his shadow walking over to the counter. This time, instead of a simple black form, his imagined shadow was a dark purple version of himself, bare-chested and with tattoos, his height, and just as thin. The shadow pulled the wooden spoon from the container, walked it over to where Jesus and Abilio sat, and put it on the table between him and his cousin. The shadow disappeared as soon as it set the spoon down—the spoon disappeared from the counter and appeared at the table.

Jesus looked at Abilio and saw his cousin staring at the space between them.

"Wha . . . What was that?" Abilio stammered.

"What was what? You mean the spoon?" Jesus said, picking the wooden spoon up from the table with pride.

"No, you, but not you. A purple you, walking around the kitchen."

Jesus felt his breath catch in his throat. "Wait, you saw that?"

Abilio looked at Jesus with wide eyes and nodded. "Can you do it again?"

After taking a big breath, Jesus picked another object on the counter—a spatula—then repeated the process he used for teleporting the wooden spoon, this time paying more attention to his shadow than to the object. His shadow stood up from where he sat, emerging from himself, before walking through the kitchen. Jesus, transfixed, forgot about the spatula, and the shadow disappeared.

"What happened?"

"I lost focus. Let me try again."

This time, Jesus kept the spatula in the back of his mind while watching the shadow version of himself in the kitchen. Then, he stood up and inspected his shadow self. In addition to the many Mayan script tattoos covering its body, the shadow also had jet-black eyes without pupils. It stood still while Jesus walked around and didn't move when Jesus passed a hand through it.

"Does it understand us?" Abilio asked, also passing a hand through the shadow's shoulder. Jesus didn't feel anything, and the shadow didn't move, but Abilio flinched like he was creeped out.

"I don't think so. It's me, but in the shadow realm."

"Can you make it do things?"

"It's how I teleport objects. So, in a way, I make it do stuff every time I teleport something."

Jesus stared at the shadow's black eyes. The shadow didn't move until Jesus thought, "Look at me," and the shadow turned its head in line with Jesus's gaze. Although it looked like something out of a horror movie, Jesus wasn't scared. In fact, he felt a paternal bond with the shadow, like he was responsible for his shadow's continued development.

Instead of carrying out the spatula's teleportation, Jesus had his shadow take the wooden spoon from the table and put it away before disappearing.

"Do you think I have a shadow form too?" Abilio asked.

"I'm pretty sure that's how it works. We'd have to ask Balam, he'd know."

"The shadow jaguar that's been around since the priests were in charge of Chichen Itza a thousand years ago—got it," Abilio said.

After realizing the time, Jesus and Abilio hurried out of the house and went to the fruit stand. Beatriz yelled at Abilio when they arrived, asking what took him so long.

Abilio looked at Jesus with a smirk, pleased with his little lie about her permission to take his time.

"You're lucky it's slow," she added before taking off her dirty apron. Despite the fruit juice stains, Jesus took it from her and hung it from his neck before tying it around his waist. She hurried away, talking about how she still had to cook for Gloria and muttering to herself the list of ingredients she'd need.

The young men sat on a pair of wooden stools while they waited for the evening's first customer. "Wait, if I can see the shadow too, does that mean everyone will also see it every time you try and teleport something?" Abilio asked.

"I don't know. Maybe you can only see it because you're Mayan?"

"Or because we were in the same building as the codices." Abilio looked at Jesus like he had a wicked idea. "Why don't we test it out, see if we can scare some of the people here."

"No way, what if they find out it's me?"

"How will they know?"

"Well, it's my shadow, so it looks like me," Jesus said, stating the obvious.

"You don't have those tattoos and stuff. Look, they'll have no idea. Just try teleporting a piece of fruit."

Jesus, still not sold with Abilio's brash idea, stared at a banana on the far side of their stand. Instead of imagining the shadow walking across the room and retrieving it, he thought it into existence right next to the banana, then popped it into place next to him. The banana ended up on his lap.

"I only saw it twice, like little blinks," Abilio reported.

"That was on purpose," said Jesus. They sat there as night fell, Jesus practicing making his shadow pop in and out of existence in the blink of an eye while transporting the banana around the stand. By the time the store got busy selling fruit smoothies to people after their dinner, Jesus could transport the banana without Abilio seeing the shadow.

Abilio turned to Jesus during a break in the customers, a little after nine at night. The streetlights around Parque de Santa Ana beat back the darkness, and all sorts of people were enjoying the warm Mexican night. "Go scare that homeless person," Abilio said with a malicious grin, gesturing towards an older man sleeping while sitting up on a bench. There were a handful of plastic tables and chairs between their fruit stand and the man.

Jesus looked around. Everyone was busy with customers of their own, or they were eating at one of the plastic tables. In short, nobody noticed them. He focused on the man and imagined his shadow appearing in front of where he sat on the bench.

Abilio hit Jesus in the arm when he saw the shadow appear, struggling to contain his laughter.

Jesus imagined his shadow standing over the homeless man, then sitting next to him, then poking him.

The man didn't respond.

A second poke proved enough for a reaction. The homeless man turned in anger towards the shadow, then tried pushing it before falling over and through the shadow when his hand didn't find anything solid. He scrambled out of the shadow, stumbled over himself, and started screaming. He ran towards the bright lights of the restaurants near the fruit stand, knocking over the plastic tables and chairs in his way.

CHAPTER THIRTEEN

"Whoa, hold it!" one of the men from the restaurant roared. The stampeding homeless man continued tearing through the empty tables and chairs, turning around every so often and looking for the shadow chasing him.

Jesus's shadow had disappeared as soon as the man took off and disrupted his concentration. Now, he couldn't take his eyes away from the commotion.

A blur of black fur streaked from the center of the park, making a beeline towards the scared man. The cat caught up to him and started batting his heels, spurring him forward.

Evading the cat distracted the scared man long enough that the restauranteur grabbed a hold of him and wrapped him in a bear hug.

"What's your problem?" he said.

"A ghost!" the homeless man said, pointing back to the bench he had been sitting on in the center of the park.

The black cat raised his hackles and hissed, reaching out and batting at the four legs in front of him.

"It's just a cat," the angry restaurant worker said. He dragged the homeless man towards the edge of the seating area and threw him down on the ground just past Jesus and Abilio's establishment. Then, he turned around and joined his fellow restauranteurs in picking up the overturned tables and chairs while apologizing to the seated diners.

The black cat disappeared in the commotion.

Jesus and Abilio leaned over the fruit stand counter and looked at the homeless man on the ground. "Are you all right?" Jesus asked. The man often lingered around the park and accepted whatever food the restaurants offered; Jesus doubted there would be any more giveaways.

The target for Jesus's prank sat on the ground and hugged his knees while rocking back and forth.

"Hey, go do that someplace else! We're running a business here!" Abilio said.

Jesus hit Abilio in the arm with the back of his hand. He exited the fruit stand, walked around the front, and put a hand on the homeless man's shoulder. "Are you all right?"

The homeless man looked at Jesus. Then, in a renewed moment of fear, his eyes opened wide, and he started crawling backward on all fours. "It was you," he said, shaking his head. Something in the alley next to the fruit stand got his attention. Jesus turned and saw the black cat.

All of a sudden, Balam transformed into the dark purple jaguar with black spots Jesus first met. His yellow eyes burrowed into the scared man.

The homeless man looked at Jesus, then at Balam, and screamed. He scrambled onto his feet and started running away, stumbling his way across the park.

Jesus turned away from the unfortunate recipient of his prank and looked back at the alley. Where the shadow jaguar stood a moment before was a small black house cat again.

"What were you thinking?" Balam said while walking up to

Jesus. They were in full view of everyone at the outdoor restaurants.

"It was his idea," Jesus whispered, pointing to Abilio.

Abilio, who had been watching the interaction with his head poking out over the fruit stand's counter, realized they were talking about him and withdrew back into the stand.

"How old are you, putting the blame on someone else?" Balam asked. "Can he use his shadow?"

"No," Jesus said, embarrassed.

"I'm assuming you told him everything," Balam said, pacing back and forth in front of Jesus.

Jesus nodded.

"Your abilities aren't some toy you can use when you're bored. They're a gift, one that a lot of your ancestors died trying to protect." Balam walked around the fruit stand and stood at the corner near the entrance.

Jesus followed with his head down. "I'm sorry," he whispered.

Balam gestured towards the swinging door with his head. Jesus walked in first, followed by the cat.

Abilio stared at the black cat in wide-eyed fascination while sitting on his wooden stool.

"Abilio, this is Balam. Balam, Abilio," Jesus said, his defeated voice betraying his disappointment in himself as he sat down.

"Nice to meet you," Abilio said.

Balam stared at Jesus's cousin until the young man turned away his gaze. "There's no time for games. You should be trying to find a way to Paris so you can get the third codex," Balam said, speaking to Jesus but looking at Abilio. "And you should be helping him. Bringing the codices back home will unlock your powers too."

Abilio perked up at the mention of his own magic. "What kind of powers do you think I'll have?"

"There's no way to tell. You might have to wait until we get all the codices back to Chichen Itza."

Abilio sighed. "Ok, so Paris . . ."

A young girl that worked at one of the other restaurants, about the same age as Abilio, approached the fruit stand from the side. Abilio stood up and met her, blocking her view of the black cat sitting inside.

"Did you have anything to do with that ghost?" she whispered.

"You don't have to be so secretive; he knows about my spells," Abilio said, gesturing to Jesus.

The young girl waited. "Well . . ."

Abilio looked at Jesus and winked. He turned back to his friend and lowered his head. "It's one of the spells I've been working on . . ."

While Abilio spun his tall tale, Jesus helped a pair of customers that arrived and ordered smoothies. He overheard portions of his cousin's story, Abilio saying that he'd used a new secret ingredient and a special process.

"I'll tell you about the spell when I perfect it," Abilio said.

Jesus snuck a look at the girl while he poured the smoothies into large glasses. She was transfixed by his cousin, staring at him with a gaze that betrayed how she hoped they could be more than mere comrades in magic. Jesus cleared his throat, and Abilio said something about needing to get back to work.

After the fruit stand customers walked away with their drinks in hand, Abilio confessed that the girl and he often shared spells they tried. "She's been obsessed with attracting money," Abilio said. "Tried all sorts of stuff. Remember that licorice smell that wafted throughout the place a few weeks ago? It was part of a spell she learned about from a santero outside the city." Abilio looked at Balam. "When the magic comes back, will the spells be more powerful?"

"Maybe? I can't be certain. This type of magic wasn't around when the priests had their power," Balam replied.

Abilio's eyes went to the top of the fruit stand, lost in a daydream of what was possible. Jesus knew the shadow guide's answer was pure politeness.

"Well, that should clear up any suspicion from you," Abilio continued, talking to Jesus. "She'll tell her mom, who will tell the other wives around here. They'll all think it was me—they already know we both believe in Santeria."

"I don't believe in it," Jesus said.

"Me and her," Abilio clarified.

A group of customers appeared at the fruit stand, and both Abilio and Jesus were called into action. Balam curled up on the floor in the corner, resting his face on his forepaws and staring at the two young men while they worked.

During a break in the rush, Balam pounced onto the wooden stool near Jesus. "This doesn't get you any closer to Paris," he said.

"I'm not going to Paris tonight," Jesus shot back. "And I'm thinking about how I can get over there. Santi won't pay for another ticket, and I already stole hundreds of dollars from Isabella."

"She'll understand," Balam said.

"Maybe, but I don't know if she'll recover."

"Still, selling fruit isn't your priority."

Jesus turned on Balam and flexed his jaw. "My family is my priority. And right now, my mother needs me here."

Balam jumped back down to the concrete floor. "Your family is more than just the people who live with you. It's every Maya in the Yucatán who had their culture ripped from their still-beating hearts."

Jesus stared at the cat, wondering how far a preachy shadow jaguar would fly when kicked.

Balam sensed he had pushed Jesus beyond his limits. "Your shadow—you can call it forth whenever you want now?"

A customer approached the stand before Jesus could answer. He waited until they left with their drink in hand.

"We realized it earlier. I was teleporting something in the house and saw it emerge from me. I still need to focus on an object though."

"It'll get easier the more you practice. Now that the second codex is back in the Yucatán, I can switch back and forth between the two forms instead of being stuck as a house cat in the light."

"I thought you said you were always the same size, that we just perceived you as a house cat."

"Well, I can make you perceive me as a shadow jaguar or a cat now. Comes in handy when scaring men who freak out when they experience magic," Balam said, referring to the scared homeless man.

Jesus smiled.

"Let me see your shadow form," Abilio said.

Jesus turned a hard gaze towards his cousin, as if Abilio had just asked someone to show him an embarrassing scar. To his surprise, Balam replied with a simple question. "Is anyone around?"

Abilio and Jesus both made sure there were no approaching customers, then Balam stood in the middle of the fruit stand. Hidden by the counters, the black cat disappeared and was replaced by the shadow jaguar. He sat down on his haunches and looked at Abilio.

"This is the coolest thing I've ever seen," Abilio said, approaching the jaguar. He reached out a hand and stroked his head. "Feels real, but cool, like plunging my hand into a refrigerator."

Jesus, having never touched Balam in shadow form either, reached out his hand. To his surprise, he saw a purple hand overlaid on his own as he reached out, as if his shadow form had a larger hand. He touched the jaguar, patting his back.

"How come our hands went through my own shadow, but I can touch yours?" Jesus asked.

"My shadow is stronger because this is my primary form," Balam said. All of a sudden, the shadow jaguar disappeared, replaced by the black cat. Balam slunk away, taking refuge in the corner again.

"Sure looks like you've perfected the spell," the girl who worked nearby said to Abilio. "That ghost jaguar looked real!"

Jesus and Abilio both shot upright. Abilio started talking before Jesus could stammer an excuse.

"Animals are easy," Abilio said. "Humans are hard. And making them move? Forget about it!" he said.

The girl looked at Abilio with doubt. "You better not be holding out on me. I share everything I learn with you," she said, turning and walking away.

"I'm not!"

She didn't turn around.

"I've never even heard of any Santeria spells working this way," Abilio added when they were alone again. "But hey, if she believes it, she won't suspect anything else."

"I shouldn't have done that," Balam said. "That was my mistake."

Abilio apologized too, for asking in the first place.

"But, we did learn something important," Balam said with a twinkle in his yellow eyes. He paused for effect, and Jesus wondered if his ancestor had taught the shadow jaguar about dramatic timing.

Balam looked at Abilio. "Your shadow form is strong enough for powers to manifest."

Abilio pretended he wasn't surprised. "Of course it is." Then, he leaned forward, curious as his nonchalant facade cracked. "How can you tell?"

"Well, the only way you could have felt my shadow form is if your shadow form was strong enough in the first place. If not, your hand would have gone through until you touched the small cat you see when I switch to the physical realm."

Abilio looked at his hands. "So my shadow is strong enough for powers . . . How do I find out what they are?"

"Just pay attention and you'll discover it soon enough," Balam said.

"Well, can you give me a hint about what's possible? So I can be on the lookout?"

"There are those who can teleport objects, like your cousin," Balam said.

"And people who can make plants grow with their touch," Jesus added.

"And, to be honest, after all the years that have gone by, there could be new emergent powers we don't even know exist yet," Balam added.

"Evolution," Jesus observed.

"Evolution?" Balam asked.

Jesus looked at the black cat and laughed. Balam knew so much about Mayan magic but didn't know anything about modern science. "I'll explain later."

Near the end of the night, when all the customers were gone and the rest of the restaurants were cleaning their tables, Balam stood up all of a sudden with his ears perked up.

"Someone's near the codices," he said.

"My mom should be coming home right about now," Jesus

said, wiping the counter while Abilio rinsed the blender pitchers.

"It's not her. There's two men," he said, darting away.

Jesus looked at Abilio, and his cousin shooed him away with the back of his hand.

"Go! I'll take care of this and come after I lock up."

CHAPTER FOURTEEN

JESUS TURNED the corner onto his block and watched as two men ran as fast as they could from his house. One of them lost a sandal in the escape, and his first barefooted step resulted in a rolled ankle. He yelped when he stumbled and fell, then scrambled on the ground away from the house. His accomplice kept running, turning the corner at the next block.

Balam, as a shadow jaguar, emerged from the house taking deliberate, stalking strides. He held his tail parallel to the ground, letting it swish like a slow, ominous metronome. Stooping down next to the discarded sandal, he nudged it with his nose.

The home invader got back onto his feet and kept retreating with a substantial limp, looking back as often as he could with eyes wide, a mixture of fear and disbelief.

By then, Jesus had caught up to Balam and stood next to the jaguar. He reached down and grabbed the sandal. "Balam protects the whole block," Jesus said, throwing the sandal at the terrified man. "And now he has your scent. Don't let him catch you anywhere near here again!"

The man picked his sandal up from the street and followed his comrade around the corner.

"I don't know if you can really smell them or not . . ." Jesus said.

"I can. I could follow them if you want, even though it's better suited for a dog," Balam said, turning his yellow eyes on Jesus. He said "dog" like the animal was beneath him.

For the first time, Jesus got the sense that the jaguar would listen to his commands. Up until then, the shadow jaguar seemed like a wise, all-knowing guide. Now, he let himself believe that Balam was more like a partner. "That's okay, I doubt they'll be coming back."

"Me too. His urine reeked of fear."

Jesus laughed. "I'd pee myself too if I saw a jaguar—especially a guard-jaguar."

"I'm guarding the codices, not the house," Balam said with a hint of defensiveness. He turned around and went back into the house, hitting Jesus on the thigh with a swish of his tail.

"I know, I know, you're not a guard dog," Jesus said with a chuckle. He followed Balam back into the house. "Did they take anything?"

"No. They were in your mother's room when I first got here as a house cat." It was Balam's turn to laugh. "I changed into my true form when their backs were turned, and they didn't notice me. One small growl and . . . you saw the rest."

Jesus inspected the front door. "How'd they get in? The lock still works." He checked the back door and found it ajar. "Someone must've forgotten to lock it." He thought back to when he was in the backyard with Abilio, before they went to the fruit stand. Abilio had followed him inside and must've left the door unlocked. "Well, at least they didn't take anything."

"Might be worth looking into a better place to store the codices instead of under your bed," Balam said. He transformed back into a black house cat, and, a moment later, Beatriz walked through the front door.

"Where's Abilio?" she said, setting down her bag on the kitchen counter. She opened it and started pulling out the dishes she had taken to Gloria's.

"Finishing up at the fruit stand," Jesus said.

Beatriz stared at Balam as he went to the back door and nudged it with his nose. Jesus opened the door for the cat, and he went out into the night.

"You've decided he's yours?" Beatriz asked. "I've seen him lingering around out back."

"More like he chose me," Jesus replied.

"Why didn't you wait for your cousin? He has all the money with him; someone could rob him."

Jesus didn't think there was any reason Beatriz should know about the break-in. Plus, how could he explain it? A shadow jaguar sensed that ancient Mayan relics were in danger?

"I really had to go to the bathroom," Jesus said, adding in a dose of fake embarrassment.

"There's a bathroom there."

"I didn't have five pesos for the attendant and didn't want to take it from the fruit stand."

Beatriz laughed. "I think the stand could afford five pesos."

"Why, when we have a perfectly good bathroom here?"

"Well, go back and walk with him," Beatriz said.

Jesus nodded and did as he was told. He found Abilio halfway home, with his headphones in, as if he didn't need a constant awareness of his surroundings while carrying the day's cash.

"Did you catch the guys?" Abilio asked when Jesus turned around next to him.

"Catch them? No way. Balam scared them off."

"Did you recognize them?" They knew most of the people in their neighborhood.

"Never seen them before. They won't be coming back—I told them that Balam guards all the houses on the block."

"Hopefully, they spread the word."

Jesus couldn't get the thought of a better storage solution from his head. He was so pensive while he got ready for bed that he forgot to remind his cousin of the importance of locking the door every time, no matter what. His dreams that night consisted of numerous thieves gathering outside his home, coming for the codices, while he and his small family held their ground. Then, he was transported into another dream, this time chasing down the men who stole the figurine from the museum, believing they had stolen the codices from him. He followed the men into a crowd and lost them in a sea of clones.

He woke up in a cold sweat in his dark bedroom. After going to the bathroom and rinsing his face, he looked at his phone and decided he would get on with his day, since it was a little before six and the sun would come out soon—plus, he doubted he could get back to sleep. He went to the museum at his normal hour and wasn't surprised when he discovered Isabella was already there.

"Can I talk to you for a second?" Jesus said, standing at her door.

"Of course," she said, folding her hands on the desk and giving him her full attention. "Did you get to rest yesterday?" she asked while he closed the door.

"A bit. I had to go to the stand and help my mom. She took dinner to Gloria."

"I should pay her a visit too," Isabella said before writing herself a note. "What did you want to talk about?"

Jesus paused for a moment, until Isabella finished writing. "I was thinking about the Dresden theft again," he began.

"I've been thinking about it a lot too," Isabella said, nodding in perceived shared sadness.

"Where would they keep something like that? I mean, instead of catching the thief at the Madrid or Paris museums, what if we looked for them where they keep the Dresden one?"

Isabella leaned back in her chair. "There are many climate-controlled places they could keep it. Think about paintings in private collections: they aren't always on display. A good place for the codex would be somewhere like that."

"Well, do you know if they're looking into those kinds of places?"

Isabella shrugged. "I know as much as you. There's not some secret museum group on Facebook where we all share updates."

Jesus laughed.

"But, to answer your question, I'm sure the police are looking into those places. I thought of those places right now, on the spot, and I don't even investigate crimes!"

Jesus thought for a moment. "Well, where else could they keep the codices? What has the right conditions?"

"Codices?" Isabella said, furrowing her brow. "There's only been one stolen."

Jesus shook his head, feeling foolish for letting the detail slip. "Right, that's what I meant, the codex."

Isabella leveled suspicious eyes at Jesus.

It was time for a hurried explanation. "I got confused because we saw the Madrid Codex too," he said.

"We did, didn't we."

Jesus knew his justification hadn't helped. If anything, Isabella seemed like she was moving the conversation forward so that Jesus wouldn't know she was suspicious. "Well, strictly from a security standpoint, a safety-deposit box at a bank would be a good place to keep one."

Jesus couldn't decide if he had imagined the emphasis on the word "one."

"Consistent temperature, away from the light. Small though, and the interior pages could develop some problems if left there for a long time."

"And anyone could get a safety-deposit box, right?" Jesus asked.

Isabella nodded while closing her eyes, as if she was disappointed in the fact.

Then, remembering her love for true crime, he started outlining the potential investigation. "Maybe the cops in Germany can look into all of the safety-deposit boxes bought around there!"

By now, Isabella's simmering resentment was obvious. She answered with a simple word, "maybe," before turning to her computer. "Like I said, these are professionals. Let's let them do their job. We should've never gone to Madrid in the first place," she said, not looking at Jesus.

Realizing his dismissal, Jesus left Isabella's office. As he went to the janitor's closet and retrieved his trusted spray bottle and rag, he thought about two things: getting a safety-deposit box and managing Isabella's suspicion. It wasn't until lunchtime that he remembered he still had another problem on his hands, one he hadn't considered since Balam had scolded him the prior evening—getting to Paris.

The one person who could afford a flight to Paris and back was the same person who'd paid for his previous trips: Santiago García, the patrón of the museum. But he wasn't a fan of Jesus, evidenced by their last encounter and everything he'd heard secondhand through Isabella, and it didn't seem like there was any way the man would bankroll a third flight.

Plus, that flight needed to be within the next few days, if

there was any hope of getting the codex back in time for the spring equinox, just seven short days away.

Jesus sighed at the prospect of another long flight. Even if he found a way without involving Santi, there was no way he could keep his job. The sole reason he was still employed after being gone for so long was that all the travel was through the museum.

If only he had Hugh's gift. One quick call and he'd be on his way.

Jesus wrung out his mop and started cleaning the entrance's floor. He stopped and held the mop upright when a thought struck him: What if his brother called Santi for him and asked for his twin's help in Paris? Did Hugh's gift still work over the phone?

Without any other options, he figured it was worth a shot. First, he needed Santi's number. It was near the end of his shift when he mustered the courage for another trip to Isabella's office. She wasn't anywhere near as cordial when he arrived as she was for his earlier visit to her office, and she made a show of being exasperated with her work.

"What?" she said.

Jesus didn't waste any time. "I need Santi's number."

Isabella laughed. "He gets mad whenever I call him. I don't even want to think about how mad he'd be if he found out I gave his number to you."

Jesus rolled his eyes. "It's not for me. Hugh asked for it. He said he's in Paris, and the museum in Mexico City wants to discuss a two-part tour for one of the exhibits there."

Isabella's eyes narrowed. "That's the kind of thing he'd talk to me about."

"Look, I don't know the details. All I know is that Hugh asked for Santi's phone number. Said it was a 'big, big opportunity.'"

Isabella studied Jesus's face. After taking a deep breath, she took out her phone. "What, are you going to memorize the number?" she said, looking at Jesus's empty hands.

"Oh, right, hold on," Jesus said, taking out his own phone.

He took down the number and left. It wasn't until after the museum closed at five that he made the call while waiting for the bus, after checking the time difference and realizing it was midnight in Paris.

Hugh answered on the third ring. "Hi, brother."

"Hey. I need a favor."

"I guessed. You never call."

Jesus heard a crowd in the background. "Where are you?"

"Outside a bar. What do you want?"

Jesus explained that he needed Hugh to call Santi and arrange a flight to Paris as soon as possible. "Tell him that you need my help."

"Man, you've really got the travel bug. But why would I do it?"

"Because I'm asking."

"There's got to be more in it for me than that."

Jesus thought for a moment. "What if I agree to help you convince Mom to move to Mexico City? You won't have to worry about her spending the money you send on me and Abilio." Even though it was a lie and he'd never talk to his mother about leaving Merida, saying the words out loud still hurt.

Hugh laughed but didn't confirm his involvement.

"Here, I have his number," Jesus continued, pulling the phone away from his ear.

"Don't bother; I already have it."

Jesus heard his brother and raised the phone back to his head.

"I'll call you back and let you know what he says," Hugh said before hanging up.

The bus pulled up, and Jesus paid his eight pesos before taking a seat. Hugh called him back when he was walking from the bus stop to the fruit stand.

"It's done. Your flight leaves tomorrow morning," Hugh said. "I'll see you in Paris."

CHAPTER FIFTEEN

BALAM DIDN'T MAKE the trip to Paris. After the break-in scare, both he and Jesus decided that staying in Merida was the best place for him so that he could keep the codices safe.

And besides, Jesus had already stolen the first two codices—how hard could the third one be? He could take care of getting it back to the Yucatán by himself, again without Balam's help.

Jesus landed in Paris in the early afternoon, and, with the help of Google Translate, got a cab straight to the Bibliothèque Nationale De France, where the Paris Codex lived, for a quick reconnaissance mission. He had found a store that had full-sized, museum-quality replicas of the codex in stock on the other side of Paris and planned on either buying or teleporting one—he preferred not to think about it as stealing—the following morning. Following that, he'd make the swap at the library and wait until his flight home.

His phone rang during the cab ride, and he shifted to his right so that he could take it out of his left pocket. Looking at the screen, he saw it was Hugh.

"Hello?"

"You make it to France all right?"

"Yes, I'm here. How'd you know I landed?"

"Who do you think set up your flight? I had Santi buy you a room in the same hotel as me too. Wait until you see this place. Are you on your way?"

"No, I'm heading to the National Library."

"You don't want to go together tomorrow?" Hugh asked. "Dennis said he'd show us around, one of his friends works there."

"I'll see it then too," Jesus replied. "I just figured it was something to do after being in the plane all day."

The phone went silent, and Jesus imagined Hugh was holding a hand over the receiver. "We'll meet you over there."

Jesus rolled his eyes. "Sure. I should be there in half an hour or so."

"Perfect. We're leaving now."

Jesus got dropped off beside the wall of a white stone building that spanned an entire block. Keeping his eyes forward and pretending he belonged there, he went inside and passed the front desk. He heard someone say something in his direction in French, but he kept his feet moving and braced for a hand on his shoulder that never came. By following the main hallway, he soon found himself in a breathtaking reading room. It had rows and rows of long desks beneath a pattern of cream-colored domes with red lines. Jesus took a seat at one of the empty chairs and took in the space, wondering which books the people around him had in front of them, before standing up and continuing his search for the codex display.

He found himself on one side of a room with stacks of collected magazines, the closest ones to him all in French, when Hugh called.

"Where are you?"

Jesus looked at the closest sign and, instead of butchering

the French pronunciation of his current room, told Hugh he'd meet him at the entrance.

Hugh and Dennis were talking to a pair of attractive young women when Jesus arrived. Jesus stood nearby and overheard Dennis say that he'd call them later that night for dinner.

"Did they come with you?" Jesus asked when the women walked away.

"No, we just met them," Dennis said. He clapped Hugh on the back. "Your brother just walked right up to them!"

Hugh smiled and shrugged.

"I couldn't find the Paris Codex," Jesus reported. He pointed to another wing of the library that he hadn't yet explored. "Maybe it's that way?"

Dennis laughed. "It's not that way," he said. "It's not any way. They don't keep it on display!"

Jesus felt the floor drop out from underneath him. He thought he'd find a room like the one in the Madrid museum, where the codex's replica was out for the public—it would make the swap easier. Now, the prospect of another swap in a small, confined space loomed ahead of him, and he imagined Hugh would be a greater distraction than Isabella and the curator in Madrid.

"Let's talk to the woman in charge."

Dennis led the way to a wing that looked more like an office building than a library. However, the same ambiance ruled the space, and it seemed to Jesus that everyone spoke in hushed tones. He couldn't imagine anyone rushing or having any arguments whatsoever. Together with his twin, he was led to a corner office.

"Knock, knock," Dennis said while knocking the open door.

The woman seated behind the desk was younger than Jesus imagined she would be after having met the curator in Madrid.

In fact, she looked like a French version of Isabella, with lighter skin and hair.

"Dennis," she said while standing up with a smile. She walked around the left side of her desk while Dennis approached and met him halfway across her office. They each put their right hand on the other's upper arm and leaned in for la bise—a kiss on each cheek.

"Sophie, I want you to meet my friends . . ."

Even though he couldn't understand French, he could tell by Dennis's body language what he had said. Jesus's heart raced while he wondered if the traditional French greeting was expected during introductions.

"Hugh."

Sophie extended her hand and shook hands with Hugh.

"And Jesus."

She said something in French while shaking Jesus's hand.

Dennis laughed while Hugh replied in French. Then, Hugh leaned closer to Jesus. "She asked if we were brothers—I told her we are twins!"

After Sophie said something else in French, Hugh told Jesus that she could tell.

Dennis rambled off in French, but Jesus heard him mention the Paris Codex—though he called it the Codex Peresianus, its French name.

Sophie shook her head and launched into an explanation.

"She said we can't see it today," Dennis told Jesus when Hugh didn't bother translating for his brother anymore. "Apparently, it's packed for moving."

"Can we see it tomorrow?"

Sophie seemed to understand the question and shook her head no. After another explanation, Dennis told Jesus that the codex was being moved off-site the next day because of construction.

Jesus almost blurted out, "Where?" but decided against it.

"Well, at least the trip wasn't a total waste," Hugh said, in French. "We got to meet the lovely Sophie," he said, taking her hand and kissing it while looking in her eyes.

Jesus thought he would throw up from seeing a version of himself attempt such blatant charm, but Sophie seemed flattered. He pulled out his cell phone and typed a sentence into the Google translation tool he still had open: "Can we see where it's packed?"

Even though he wouldn't be able to see the codex, knowing where it was seemed like an integral part of his teleportation. It was how he had taken Isabella's credit card, even though he hadn't seen it, and if he could pull off this heist, he wouldn't have to worry about the codex's discovery—nobody would open the box until at least the next day, and in all likelihood much longer.

Sophie looked confused when Jesus held up his phone with the translation. "Why?" she said.

Jesus typed into his phone again. He felt the heat of Hugh's stare on the side of his face.

"I'm interested in how you transport treasured documents."

Sophie said, "Ah," while lifting her head, showing she understood, before launching into a lengthy statement.

"She said the planning took her months because the Paris Codex is so damaged. She's actually proud of the work and would love to show off the arrangement she came up with."

While Dennis translated, Sophie looked up something on her computer and locked it before ushering the three men from her office. Then, she told a woman at the desk outside of her office that she'd be back in a little while.

Jesus, Hugh, and Dennis followed Sophie two levels belowground. She led them down an industrial hallway, and they ended up outside a large green metal door. Unlocking it required both a key card and a retinal scan.

"Nobody's going to steal this one," Hugh joked, in French.

Sophie remarked on the sad situation in Dresden, saying it was a dark moment for their community.

Jesus understood "Dresden" but nothing else.

Sophie led them into a long underground warehouse that extended far into the distance. Exposed wiring on the ceiling led to simple gunmetal hanging light fixtures, dozens per aisle. Sophie marched past numerous rows of tall shelves before turning into an open space.

There were dozens of stainless steel boxes the size of large luggage in piles as tall as Dennis, the tallest member of their group. Humming with electricity, the cases were stacked on each other so that the longest part of the box faced them, and in the center of each box was a black card etched with a white number. Sophie started inspecting the various numbers, leading them past the entire first row. She made a right and started on the second row.

"I think it's around here," she said, her eyes working down the stack halfway through the row. She put an index finger on the correct box. "It's right here."

Jesus typed into his phone, then held it up for Sophie. "So there's no way we can see it?"

Sophie shook her head and laughed. She started into an explanation about how much each box weighed, how they used forklifts for stacking them, and about the technology in each box that kept damaged documents like the Paris Codex safe.

Jesus didn't hear any of it despite Dennis translating bits and pieces. Instead, he was focused on blinking his shadow into existence, grabbing the document, and putting it into his backpack. A lot of his energy went into what would happen once the codex got into his backpack, since it was all the luggage he had brought with him and it was rather full at the moment—he hadn't gone to the hotel, so all of his clothes were crammed inside. He imagined his shadow sliding the codex into the built-in pocket for a computer with care, creating space by compressing his clothes.

By focusing on the document's physical characteristics on the other side of the container wall and imagining the Mayan script written on the pages, Jesus thought that the codex would appear in his backpack, just like Isabella's credit card had in her office. Except, no matter how hard he focused, he couldn't sense the document; his shadow was like a dog whose owner pretended to throw a ball but in fact kept it in his hand. It surprised him that he could be so close to such a large reserve of ancient power without feeling even a trace of magic.

Sophie saying something about "magnétique" as she tapped the side of the box pulled Jesus from his thoughts. The word, in Spanish, was "magnética." Then, he understood: his magic wasn't powerful enough to get past the magnetic field in the box. Rather, the magnetic field was stopping him from tapping into the codex's magic, and without help from the codices now in the Yucatán or the land itself, he didn't have enough for the teleportation. His chance for taking the codex was gone; it would be somewhere else tomorrow, and he'd have to wait until another equinox to bring magic back to the Maya.

Unless he could find more magic . . . Jesus looked around while Sophie kept talking. He took a step backwards while leaning back so he could look over a broader area. Then, he saw it: a box cutter, abandoned on a nearby shelf.

The one way he could get enough power to get past the magnetic field was the same way he got the Dresden Codex in the first place: blood magic.

"What are you doing?" Hugh asked. He masked his anger with a smile, but Jesus could tell.

Jesus started walking towards the box cutter while Hugh hissed his name.

"Jesus?" Sophie said. Jesus put a hand on the shelf, covering the box cutter, and turned around.

"Bathroom?" he said.

Sophie pointed in the opposite direction.

An apologetic Jesus pocketed the box cutter, then hurried past the three people staring at him. He lost no time getting into the bathroom—so he wouldn't forget the codex's location among the containers—and took off his backpack, emptying it on the floor. He had to focus on getting past the magnetic field and didn't want to worry about finding space among his clothes.

Holding the box cutter in his right hand, he looked down at his left. He held the blade between his left thumb and forefinger, took a deep breath, and swiped.

He sensed the power emanating from the codex the instant the first drop of blood spilled. While focusing on the codex's physical qualities with his eyes closed, he imagined his shadow taking the codex, bringing it to the bathroom, and putting it into his backpack.

His backpack was still empty on the ground when he opened his eyes. This wasn't how it was supposed to work!

Jesus sensed he was out of time and out of options. If Balam was there . . . Jesus shook his head. Balam wasn't there, and he was on his own. All he could think about was more magic. And that meant more blood.

He looked down at his left wrist. A quick swipe, not enough to kill him, just enough for more blood. His last resort.

Holding the blade against the left side of his wrist, he made a quick slash and held his hand over the sink. The combination of the surge of power and loss of blood made him dizzy, and he clutched the counter for support.

He imagined his shadow reaching through the metal box's

magnetic field, thought about the texture of the folded pages against his fingers, believed he could smell the paper and preservation chemicals fighting the years of decay. Then, his shadow was in the bathroom with him, putting the codex into his backpack with care.

Jesus felt himself losing consciousness when he heard a knock on the door.

"Jesus, what's taking so long?" yelled Hugh.

Jesus half lowered, half collapsed onto the ground. The last thing he saw was the Paris Codex sitting inside his open backpack.

CHAPTER SIXTEEN

SLOW BEEPING CREEPED into Jesus's awareness. He got the sense that he had just left a dream, but he couldn't remember what it was about. When the beeping didn't stop, he realized that it was coming from somewhere outside himself. His eyelids peeled open, and the fluorescent light overhead burned his eyes before he closed them again.

"What—" he croaked, no louder than a whisper. His voice was hoarse, ragged, and his throat hurt when he swallowed.

The beeping came from his left. He turned his head, forced his eyes open, and saw the machine that made the steady, continuous sound; it came from a square screen on a thin pole. Beyond, the window showed the black of night with thin tendrils of dawn or dusk seeping through.

Jesus returned his head to the pillow and took deep breaths. He was in the hospital. The last thing he remembered . . .

Hugh. And the Paris Codex.

He moved his hands, wondering if he was in handcuffs after the theft. Despite his pervasive weakness, he got both of them onto his stomach and didn't feel anything holding him in place. But he did feel his left wrist, then his left hand; they were wrapped in gauze and ached in spite of the drugs coursing through his body.

Many minutes passed while Jesus got his bearings. His heart raced when he wondered how long he had been out, knowing a long stay in a Paris hospital meant he would miss the coming equinox.

With a mighty surge of effort, Jesus propped himself onto one elbow and looked at the room around him. Sitting on a chair in the corner, her head resting on her hand, was a sleeping Beatriz.

A wave of light-headedness forced Jesus's head back down to the pillow. His mother, in Paris? How did she get there? Did Hugh pay for the flight?

And what happened to the codex?

Jesus spoke after another gathering of effort. "What are you doing here?" It came out a jumbled string of sounds.

Beatriz stirred, rearranging herself, but didn't wake up.

"Mom," Jesus said louder, ignoring his sore throat.

Beatriz's eyes fluttered open, and she lifted her head from her hand. She looked at her son and, realizing he was awake, rushed to his side.

"Shh," she said, stroking his arm. "Rest. You've had a long trip."

Another wave of confusion. He'd had a long trip? "How did you get here?" Jesus said. He licked his cracked lips with a dry tongue.

"I asked the neighbor to drive me," Beatriz replied. "The buses haven't started for the day yet."

Jesus digested the information before asking where they were.

"In Merida. Hugh brought you back from Paris after your accident," she said. "Hold on, let me get the nurse. She wanted to know when you woke up."

Jesus reached out for Beatriz's arm but grabbed nothing but air. A few minutes later, the nurse followed Beatriz into the hospital room and approached the IV drip. "You need to rest," she said.

Before Jesus could object, he felt a wave of exhaustion take over him. He tried spilling out more questions but instead fell asleep without saying another word.

The sun was out when he woke up again. Although he didn't want to admit it, he did feel better after his forced rest. Beatriz stood up and walked back to his side when he propped himself on an elbow.

"How do you feel?" she said, as if she could tell her son was feeling better than the first time he woke up.

"Fine," Jesus said. "Where's Hugh?" he asked—the question on his mind before he passed out.

"He went back to Mexico City. Said he had urgent business."

"Did he say anything about . . . my stuff?"

"He left it here," Beatriz said, pointing to the ground next to the window.

Jesus leaned over and pointed to his bag. "Can you bring it here?"

Beatriz nodded. "Sure. What do you want?"

Jesus had no energy left for secrets. If she found the codex . . . . well, he'd just have to tell her the truth.

Beatriz plopped the bag on Jesus's bed. The movement sent a shot of pain through his left forearm, and he flexed his jaw in response.

"What do you need?" Beatriz said while unzipping his bag.

"Is there anything that looks like it belongs in a museum?" he replied.

She shoved aside his clothes and shook her head. "In here?"

she asked as if she was playing along with his delusions. "I don't see anything."

"What about in the pocket for a computer?" Jesus said. Speaking brought his immense thirst to the front of his awareness.

Beatriz shook her head, and Jesus got the sense she was treating him like a small child. "Nothing in there," she said, shoving the clothes back down and zipping the backpack closed.

Of course Hugh took the codex.

"Where's my phone?" Jesus asked.

Beatriz put the backpack back below the window before going back to a small locker near her chair. While her back was turned, Jesus reached out for the glass of water on his nightstand.

When Beatriz turned back around with the phone in hand and saw her son reaching for the cup, she hurried to his side and grabbed it for him.

"You just lay back and rest. I'm here," she said, holding out the glass of water.

Jesus took it and took a drink, spilling some on his chest. Beatriz handed him his phone.

It was dead.

Defeated, Jesus laid his head back on his pillow.

"What's wrong?" Beatriz asked, the concern apparent in her voice.

"My phone's dead. There's a charger in my bag—can you grab it?"

After his mother plugged in his phone, Jesus asked, "Can you call Hugh?"

Beatriz pulled her own phone from her pocket and dialed the number. Then, she held the phone up to her ear.

"Hunahpu, did you make it home safe?"

"Good."

"Oh, he's good. Just woke up and asked me to call you."

Jesus held out his hand.

"He wants to talk to you."

"Ok. But remember, he just woke up."

Beatriz held out the phone.

"Hey, brother, how are you feeling?" Hugh said when Jesus got on the phone.

"Where is it?"

"Where is what?"

"Don't play with me. You know what I'm talking about."

"Look, we were all very worried about you. I have to call Dennis and Sophie as soon as we get off the phone—she had to take the rest of the day off work because she was so upset."

"Where's the codex?" Jesus said, tired of the gaslighting.

"The codex? It's probably going to the storage facility, like Sophie said . . ."

"I saw it in my backpack before I passed out."

Hugh's tone turned sad. "Your backpack was empty when I broke the door getting into the bathroom. Your stuff was thrown everywhere, and you were on the ground, surrounded by your own blood."

Imagining the situation, Jesus felt his resolve crack.

Hugh continued. "Put yourself in my shoes. Finding your own brother like that wasn't easy."

Jesus muttered an apology.

"And now you're calling, grilling me about an old document that belongs to a museum in Paris. I think the drugs are getting to your head."

Jesus shook his head. "No, no, I know what I saw."

"That somehow the codex ended up in your backpack while you were in the bathroom? Think about what you're saying, Jesus. It makes no sense."

Jesus opened his mouth but couldn't form an explanation.

"You don't really believe it, do you?" Hugh asked.

Jesus couldn't explain why, or how, but he started second-guessing what he saw while he was on the bathroom floor.

"So, you didn't see anything in my backpack?"

"No, it was empty."

Jesus let his arm relax and the phone rested on the pillow. He could still hear Hugh talking.

"Now, I don't want you to worry about the hospital bill. I'll take care of everything. You just focus on getting better," his twin said.

Jesus nodded. Then, when he realized his brother couldn't hear a nod, he said, "All right." A thought occurred to him. "Wait, how come I made it back to Merida without remembering anything?"

"Sedatives. I didn't want you freaking out. But it sounds like they gave you some wild ideas," Hugh said with a laugh.

Jesus flexed his jaw in anger. "They aren't wild ideas," he said.

Hugh sighed. "Look, don't mention ancient relics appearing out of thin air to anyone else, okay? They'll think you're crazy." With that, Hugh hung up the phone. His words cut through everything Jesus thought he knew, making him second-guess the existence of the two codices hidden under his bed—a magic spell sowing doubt. Did Balam even exist, or was it a dream?

Despite knowing Hugh's gifts, Jesus couldn't shake the unease he felt from wondering if he made everything up. There was one way he could know for sure: he could teleport an object, or call forth his shadow form. He focused on a box of rubber gloves, imagining his shadow taking one, bringing it across the room, and putting it in his hand . . .

"Do you need anything else?" Beatriz asked, dashing Jesus's focus.

"No, I'm fine. Shouldn't you be at the fruit stand?"

"No, I woke Abilio up when Hunahpu first called and told him he's going to be on his own today."

"All day?"

"Don't worry, I called Vicente and told him to keep an eye on him," Beatriz said with a sly grin. Vicente ran one of the nearby restaurants.

Jesus laid his head back against the pillow and shut his eyes. He felt like he'd been discovered by his brother, not as the thief who stole the codices, and not as the man who would bring back magic to the Mayan people, but as a delusional pretender caught up in a story where he was the hero.

He tried conjuring his shadow form again but realized he couldn't—Beatriz's presence didn't allow for concentration. But she had to go to the bathroom at some point, and that's when he would make his move and prove to himself that he wasn't making it all up. He just had to wait.

Isabella arrived before Beatriz left Jesus alone. The nurse led her in, and for the first few minutes of her visit she talked to Beatriz about life, catching up over Gloria and the death of Flaco. Then, she approached Jesus.

"How are you doing?" she asked.

"I've been better," Jesus said, lifting his bandaged left arm.

Isabella put a hand on his forearm and guided it back down to the bed.

"Santi told me you were needed in Paris. How was the trip?" Her words hung in the air for a moment before she added, "Other than the obvious problems."

Jesus felt a wave of guilt wash over him. Isabella didn't act like anything was amiss. "The trip was good. Hugh needed me out there."

"So I heard. And he's the one that brought you back, right?" Isabella said, turning to Beatriz.

Beatriz nodded.

"She called you?" Jesus asked.

"To let me know you wouldn't be coming into work for a few days, at least. She didn't know Santi already told me that you were coming back next week, so I didn't even expect you back anyways."

Beatriz put her hands on her knees and stood up. "Since you're here to sit with him, I'm going to run to the bathroom," she said, leaving the room.

"You don't have to stay with me," Jesus told Isabella once they were alone, as much for her sake as his own. The guilt was eating him from the inside.

"Someone does," Isabella said, her tone frosty without Beatriz in the room.

Jesus looked at her with inquisitive eyes while tilting his head.

Isabella gestured towards Jesus's bandaged wrist and Jesus understood: they thought he was trying to kill himself, and the two women had just handed over the reins of his suicide watch.

"Look, it's not what you think," Jesus said, searching for an explanation.

"To be honest, I don't know what to think," Isabella said. She started pacing at the foot of his bed.

Jesus asked her, "What's wrong?" when she didn't continue.

"Look, now might not be the best time to say anything, but I know you stole my credit card and ordered a replica of the Madrid Codex."

Jesus took a calming breath, but she continued before he could utter a word.

"I don't know where it is, or what you did with it, but it's hundreds of American dollars gone. So, not only did I not get to go to Paris, I also lost serious money." Her words poured out in a flurry. "And, I know this isn't a good time, but I don't know if there will ever be a good time, so I'm just going to say it: don't bother coming back to the museum. I won't bother you for the money—your poor mother's been through enough—and we'll pretend we just went our separate ways."

Isabella cut Jesus off when he opened his mouth to speak. "You hurt me, Jesus, even after all I did for you." She looked at the hospital room door. "Beatriz should be back soon—don't do anything stupid while you're alone. I need some fresh air.

"Goodbye, Jesus." She left the room without looking at him again.

Jesus, still stunned by the news that he had been fired, realized a moment later that he now had the opportunity to call forth his shadow form, teleport an object, and prove to himself—and Hugh—that it wasn't all in his head.

He focused on the box of gloves, paying attention to the shape, color, and smell of latex. When he got a hold of the object, he imagined his shadow leaving him and approaching the box before bringing it to his side.

The shadow never appeared. He tried numerous times while Beatriz was in the bathroom, and, no matter what he did, he couldn't generate even a hint of a shadow, let alone teleport an object.

His magic was gone. And, what's worse, he wasn't sure it ever even existed.

CHAPTER SEVENTEEN

CONVINCING Beatriz that she could leave him alone had taken the entire afternoon. Part of his justification was that Abilio was alone for the Thursday night crowd—the first of three consecutive nights each week where the fruit stand made most of its money.

"If Abilio takes too long, the customers could go somewhere else," he had said.

Beatriz had crossed her arms while settling into the chair. "Well then, they'll just have to wait. But he can go fast when he has to."

"Come on, I'll be fine here. There are nurses right outside the door I can call; they can help me with whatever I need."

Beatriz had been unfazed.

"And what's going to happen when I leave? Are you going to be with me all the time, even at work?" Jesus hadn't told her about losing his job yet.

"If I have to," his mother said, raising her stubborn eyebrows.

In the end, what broke her iron resolve was a believable lie.

"I'm just going to sleep anyways. What are you going to do, watch me breathe?"

"Maybe," she had replied.

"Look, the sun's down. Go help Abilio so I can rest without worrying about him. You can pick me up on Saturday morning, when they said I can go."

Beatriz's hardened demeanor broke, and she had walked to her son's side. "Always worrying about others," she had said, stroking his hair.

Jesus pulled away. "Go, I'll be fine."

"I'll have my cell phone on me. Call if you need anything," she had said before walking out the door.

As soon as she left, Jesus tried conjuring his shadow form again. He focused on various objects around the room, as light as a piece of tissue and as heavy as a clipboard, and, no matter what he did, his shadow form never sprang forth.

Struggling under the weight of defeat, he stared out into the night. A sudden thought occurred to him, and he reached out for his phone on the nightstand.

"When you get home, can you check that everything is safe under the bed?" he texted to Abilio.

The reply came right away. "Sure." The fruit stand must not be too busy.

There was nothing for Jesus to do but wait. At some point, he fell asleep.

"Wake up," a deep voice said.

Jesus stirred, then opened his eyes. He didn't remember a male doctor or nurse, but maybe one's shift had just started.

The room was empty.

Jesus blinked twice, wondering if the voice was in a dream.

"We have a problem," the same deep voice said from the left side of his bed.

Jesus turned, leaned over the edge, and saw the shadow

jaguar. Balam. His dark purple head came up to the side of his mattress.

He felt like leaping down and wrapping his arms around the creature, grateful he hadn't made him up. "Wait, why can I see you? My magic doesn't work anymore otherwise."

"There are too many drugs in your system. Let them pass and you'll be fine," Balam said. He paced between the window and the bed, agitated. "Hugh has the Paris Codex in Mexico City."

Jesus felt a surge of anger originate in his gut and course through his body. "I knew it! He made me think I was crazy."

"There was a priest at Chichen Itza who used his gift in much the same way; the other priests replaced him on the ruling council."

"He took it from me when I was passed out in Paris."

"I felt it as soon as he landed in Merida; I followed him to Mexico City. Now that all four codices are back in Mexico, I can travel through the shadow realm again. I came back as soon as I saw where he put it."

"Which is . . ."

"In a bag he keeps with him at all times."

Jesus laid his head back on his pillow. "So, there are two in Merida, and two in Mexico City."

"And only three days before the equinox."

Jesus pulled out his phone and looked up the price for flights from Merida to Mexico City and back. Realizing there was no way he could afford one, he instead checked for bus tickets. "It's a twenty-one-hour bus ride from here to Mexico City. The next one leaves tomorrow morning."

"Can you get to Chichen Itza in time?"

Jesus looked up the exact moment of the spring equinox: 9:32 in the morning. Going back to the tab with the bus routes, he found that he could get from Mexico City to Chichen Itza in a little over twenty-two hours. "It'll be close—we have to be in and out."

"I doubt Hugh will make it easy for you."

"You'll be there, won't you? We'll just scare him; no way he's going to stand up to a jaguar."

"And what about the rest of the security? Do you think they'll let you just get on a bus and ride back to the Yucatán?"

Jesus thought for a moment. "We can worry about that later. First things first, let's just get to Mexico City."

Balam transformed into a black house cat and disappeared under Jesus's bed as the room's door opened and a nurse walked in. She asked Jesus how he was feeling, wrote something on the chart at the foot of his bed, and left.

The shadow jaguar reappeared. "You might need some help," Balam said, pointing to Jesus's bandaged wrist and hand with his snout.

"I think I'll be all right," Jesus said, lifting the arm. He tried flexing his hand and winced.

Balam stared at him.

"All right, maybe, but who can I ask?"

"Bring your cousin."

"Abilio? He has to work at the fruit stand."

Balam shook his head. "You have a few hours in Mexico City to grab two codices so you can bring magic back. What if they're not in the same place when we get there? You might have to split up in order to get them both in time."

Balam was right. Still, Jesus took a deep breath and sighed before admitting the fact. "All right, let me send him a message." He told Abilio they were going to Mexico City tomorrow and to not tell Beatriz that Jesus was going too.

"Then what should I tell her?" Abilio replied right away.

"Say that Hugh bought you a ticket that leaves tomorrow. We'll be there for less than a day."

"Less than a day after that long ride! Fine, ok, hold on."

Jesus told Balam what Abilio had texted.

Jesus's phone buzzed with another text from Abilio. "She said she's excited for me."

"She didn't care about you leaving her alone?"

"She said that she left me alone, so we're even." He finished the text with a smiley face.

"Meet me at the bus station at eight tomorrow morning; don't be late," Jesus said, sending him the address.

Abilio gave Jesus a thumbs-up.

Jesus told Balam that Abilio was in.

"Good. You should get some rest—we have a rough few days ahead of us," Balam said. He transformed back into the house cat and retreated under Jesus's bed.

"Shouldn't you be guarding the codices?" Jesus asked.

Balam, from under the bed, replied, "They're in the ring of cenotes, so I can sense them from here."

Jesus hadn't heard of any ring before, so he looked it up on his phone. The ring is at the edge of the Chicxulub crater, made when an asteroid hit eons ago—the same asteroid that killed the dinosaurs.

The night dragged by with Jesus passing in and out of sleep. His alarm went off at five a.m. plenty of time for escaping the hospital and getting to the bus station—and he silenced the phone in his hand, since he was already awake.

Jesus waited for the nurse's next visit with nervous anticipation. When he heard his door creaking open, he pretended that he was asleep. She stood at the foot of his bed for less than a minute before leaving and closing the door behind her with a gentle click.

As soon as he heard the sound, Jesus sat up and sprang into action. He took off his hospital gown and put on some of the clothes he had packed for his trip to Paris; the clothes he wore when he passed out from blood loss were gone.

He shuddered when he thought about how much blood must have been on them, and a small part of him felt bad for Hugh.

Balam emerged from beneath the bed and retook his form as a shadow jaguar. "I'll meet you outside. Nobody wants to see a cat walking through a hospital."

"And now that you can teleport—"

"Travel through the shadow realm," Balam corrected.

"There's no reason for you to stick with me," Jesus said, teasing the cat. It was the first time he'd thought of Balam as a friend.

"Do you want me to stick with you?" Balam asked, his tone serious.

"No, no, I was just joking." Jesus slung his backpack over his shoulders. "I'll see you outside."

There was one movie he had seen years ago, he couldn't remember the name, about a bedridden man who escaped the hospital on a rolling bed using a mop while being chased by a man with a gun. If that guy could get out of the hospital, he could, even if he was supposed to be in there for a few more days.

Jesus poked his head out of the room's door and looked both ways. He found the stairwell in the distance and was about to emerge from his room when he saw the nurse leaving a room down the hall. After pulling his head back into his room, he listened to the retreating footsteps, waiting until they disappeared. Then, he checked the empty hall once more and ran to the stairwell.

Taking the steps two at a time was a bad idea. At the first landing, he felt light-headed and had to grab onto the railing before he fell over. From there, he went down the remaining three levels with both hands on the railings and using every step. At the ground floor, he opened the door and peeked into the lobby.

A security guard, an older man with white hair and a drab, loose-fitting gray button-down shirt, stared at him, questioning him with his eyes. Jesus withdrew back into the stairwell. Then, he strode out of the stairwell with his head held high, radiating confidence.

The guard didn't take his eyes off of him. Jesus wondered when the man would call the authorities and prepared for a run through the entrance.

"Your wristband is still on," the guard said.

Jesus, startled, looked down and saw it. He looked back at the guard, who was holding out a pair of scissors. He approached the desk and cut off his wristband.

"I'm not here to keep people in; I have to keep people out," the guard said with a broad smile.

Jesus mumbled his thanks and walked through the automatic doors. With a black cat at his heels, he walked to the closest bus stop so he could take the bus to where he would meet Abilio.

His cousin was waiting for him at the depot. The attendant scanned their tickets, and they waited at the curb with the rest of the passengers and their luggage until the bus pulled up.

Their seats were at the back of the bus. Jesus counted himself lucky that he had made sure that they were sitting together—another pair of friends hadn't made sure their tickets were adjacent and each ended up next to strangers.

"Might as well settle in; we're going to be here for a while," Abilio said when the bus started moving.

Jesus took his backpack off his lap and set it between his feet. Then, he unzipped the top, and Balam poked his head through.

"I was about to ask where he'd been," Abilio whispered. He reached down and scratched the cat's head. Jesus thought he saw a hint of a purple shadow around his cousin's hand.

"He could teleport now that all four codices are here in Mexico, but he wanted to stick with me."

Balam had taken Jesus's joke to heart.

"So, are we going to see Hugh?" Abilio asked as they passed through Merida's city limits.

"That's the plan." Jesus then told him all that had happened in Paris, and that the last two codices were in Mexico City with Hugh.

"That guy," Abilio said, shaking his head.

"What?"

"I know you two don't get along."

"We get along just fine."

Abilio shrugged. "Doña Beatriz says that you never forgave him for yelling at her."

"It's not just that. We're just . . . different."

A long time passed while Abilio stared out the window. He turned back to Jesus. "She doesn't need you to protect her from him, you know."

Jesus sighed. "I know. It's not just that."

When Jesus didn't continue, Abilio opened his eyes and jutted his head forward—he wanted more information.

"When our dad left, Mom was all alone," Jesus said, staring past his cousin, remembering. "She was involved in church before, but then she dove in.

"Well, one Sunday, the priest cornered us—I don't know where Hugh was. He started talking about how a good Christian woman should be able to keep a man and said reckless women wouldn't be allowed at his church."

"Father Ramirez said that?" Abilio said, scandalized.

Jesus nodded. "I didn't say a word, just stood there while he made my mom cry."

Abilio tapped Jesus's thigh. "You were just a kid. Nothing you could do."

"But I wasn't a kid when Hugh yelled at her."

Abilio lifted his chin while opening his mouth. "Makes sense."

"I felt the same way as I did all those years ago. Like I can't protect my mom."

"I'm sure she doesn't feel that way," Abilio said.

Jesus ignored his cousin's comment. "And I guess I just get mad at Hugh because he doesn't make her life any easier."

CHAPTER EIGHTEEN

"WE'RE HERE," Jesus said, shaking Abilio awake.

His cousin perked up and looked out the window. The bus depot in Mexico City was indistinguishable from the one they'd left behind in Merida almost a full day before, except here, the sun wasn't up. Abilio wiped the drool from his chin with the back of his hand and scratched his head.

"That wasn't so bad," Abilio said. It was a lie, and both he and Jesus knew it—their complaints had started at the rest stop that designated the halfway point. Worse, they had a few hours before they got on another bus that would take them a mere hour from where they had come from in the first place.

They disembarked the bus—with Balam in the now zipped-up backpack—and asked an attendant for help getting to the National Museum of Anthropology, where the Mexico City codex resided. The woman hadn't heard of it before, so she looked it up on her phone.

"Oh, it's across the street from the zoo!" Having been there with her children, she told them the fastest way was taking a cab.

"Or, if you want, there's a bus that just started running," she said, looking at her watch.

Jesus checked the time on his phone; it was minutes after five in the morning. He asked for the bus route, and she gave him the instructions.

"Takes about an hour," the woman added. Jesus thanked her and walked away with his cousin.

"Our bus leaves from here at eleven," Jesus said while they waited at the bus stop. "So we need to be on our way back here by ten at the latest. If we can get the first codex quickly, we should have enough time to go to Hugh's place and get the Paris Codex before coming back."

Jesus felt his backpack wiggling. He set it on the ground and unzipped the top.

Balam jumped out and shook, starting at his nose and ending at his tail.

Another passenger on the bus from Merida, an older man and the sole person also waiting for the Mexico City bus, looked at the cat in horror.

Jesus and Balam walked away, leaving Abilio leaning on the bus shelter.

"I'll go ahead of you to the museum, see if there's a way we can get in," Balam said. He transformed into his full shadow jaguar form and stretched.

Jesus looked back at the waiting man and saw him staring at Balam. When he didn't turn his gaze, Jesus positioned his body so that he was blocking the man's view.

"Wait," Jesus said, before Balam could leave. "If you can teleport there, why don't you just teleport inside and steal it?"

Balam shook his powerful cat head. "Can't." He lifted up a paw. "What will I grab it with?"

"You could put it in your mouth."

Balam laughed. "Even if I got past whatever security

measures they have protecting the codex, I can't fold it up with my snout."

"Well, what if it's already folded? You never know."

"Could be. How can I explain this . . ." Balam paused, as if he was thinking. "In order to lift the object in physical space, I'd have to be a small cat." He transformed back into the black cat and opened his mouth wide. "Much too small," he said. Then, he transformed back into his shadow form. "And in the shadow realm, my teeth would tear it before it budged."

"None of them have been that heavy," Jesus countered. He thought about how light the codices seemed in his backpack.

"To you! Your primary form is in the physical realm, so the codices exist for you there."

"Why do they seem lighter when picked up? It even happened to Isabella," Jesus asked, thinking back to when she'd picked up his bag with the codex inside at the airport.

"Shadow form's lifting some of the weight. She's Mayan, I'm guessing?"

Jesus nodded.

"See, her shadow form resonated with the codex, making it lighter. That won't happen to non-Maya."

"So it'll be heavier than normal for them?"

"Not by much. They would experience it in the physical realm, because the power doesn't exist for them."

Jesus nodded his head as if he understood, but it still didn't make much sense to him. Balam seemed convinced though, and he said he'd see them there before disappearing.

The bus pulled up a few minutes after Balam left. The other passenger that boarded with Jesus and Abilio made sure he took a seat as far away as possible from the pair.

"Hugh's not going to just give us the other codex," Abilio said, keeping the volume of his voice low.

"I know."

"So are you going to fight him for it?"

"I don't think it will come to that. I'll just walk in with Balam in his full shadow form—no way he'll want to stand up to a jaguar."

"What if he does?"

"Well then, I'll just teleport the codex into my backpack and we'll run away."

"Run," Abilio said with a chuckle. "You mean go to the bus stop, wait, go to another bus, then sit for a day on the way back."

The bus dropped them off outside the zoo as the sun cleared the horizon. They walked up Calle de Acuario and turned left onto Paseo de la Reforma.

The National Museum of Anthropology was on their right.

It didn't open until ten.

"Ten!" Abilio said. "That's when we need to be on our way back to the bus depot!"

"I know, I know," Jesus said, pacing.

"Maybe you can buy a flight back, so we can have more time."

"I don't have enough money for that."

"Can't you teleport some?"

Jesus looked at Abilio with a stern gaze. "I'm just saying . . ." Abilio muttered.

"Look, it's a little after six now. Maybe if we go to Hugh now, get the Paris Codex, we can come back here when it opens."

"Or . . . we can find a way into this place. Stealing the codex might be easier without anyone else there," Abilio said with a healthy dose of mischief in his eyes.

"Agreed," Balam said, appearing from behind a nearby bush. "In fact, I already found a way inside."

Jesus felt a weight leave his shoulders. He was so happy that he could hug Balam, but he had a feeling the shadow jaguar wouldn't appreciate the gesture.

"Follow me, and stay hidden," Balam said. He led them around the grounds of the building, sticking to the trees surrounding the parking lot. Jesus saw security cameras at the corners and on the walls. "We'll have to be quick," he said.

"It's behind a pane of thick glass, but you shouldn't have a problem," Balam said, his tail swishing behind him.

Jesus felt a swell of pride at the shadow jaguar's confidence in him. But his magic didn't work at the hospital . . . what if it still hadn't come back?

Balam stopped when they were on the side of the building opposite the main street. "See that door?" he said, pointing with his nose.

Both Jesus and Abilio nodded.

"The cleaning crew left out of there when I first got here. Push a bar on the other side and it opens, no alarm."

"How do you know there's no alarm?" Abilio asked.

"I might have scared the person before they set it," Balam said.

"What if they called someone to check out the jaguar in the museum?" replied Abilio. "Maybe they thought it escaped from the zoo!"

"Because I wasn't a jaguar. I was a small cat. And I let him chase me out—he never went back in and set the alarm."

Jesus laughed. "That's one way to do it."

"So are you two ready?" Balam asked. He teleported without waiting for an answer.

A moment later, the door in the distance nudged open. Jesus and Abilio scurried across the access street and ran inside.

"The cameras probably saw us," Jesus said, his heart racing.

"Then we'll have to be quick," answered Abilio.

Balam led them through the museum to the room that held

the Maya Codex of Mexico. It was unfolded on a large display table, surrounded by a glass case. Early morning sunlight filtered down through windows high overhead and fell on Mayan and Aztec sculptures against the walls.

"Work your magic, cousin," Abilio said.

Jesus rubbed his hands together, playing the part. In truth, he was terrified. He hadn't used his magic since before the hospital, and he wasn't 100 percent convinced it would work the way it had before. Jesus focused on the codex, starting at the edges and letting every character written on the ancient document wash over his awareness. In his imagination, his shadow form left his body and approached the codex.

Relief flooded through his veins when he saw his shadow form appear in reality. It looked larger than before, as if it had gone through a second puberty. It was a little taller than him, with thick arms and legs. The Mayan script tattoos covering his body were darker than night, absorbing all light around them.

"You've been working out," Abilio whispered in awe.

"All four codices are back in Mexico now, and he's standing near one," Balam said.

Jesus shushed both of them. In his mind, his shadow folded the codex, carried it towards him without any regard for impediments, and put it in his backpack.

Just like every other time.

Except this time, nothing happened. The codex stayed put, separated from them by the pane of glass.

"I didn't think that would work," a voice said from the shadows on the far side of the room.

Jesus knew the voice right away.

Hugh.

"I whispered to the glass, told it not to let you take the codex. Just in case I couldn't stop you."

Abilio gasped. "A real spell," he said, in awe.

"Look, Hugh, you need to let me take this. There's more at stake than you realize."

"I don't need to do anything," Hugh said, stepping into the light. He stood on the opposite side of the spread-open codex, staring at Jesus, Abilio, and Balam with a sneer on his face and a leather messenger bag slung over his shoulder. His eyes were bloodshot, and his disheveled hair was greasy.

"That's a cool trick. When did you realize you could do that?" Hugh said, pointing to Balam.

"I'm not some trick," Balam said, spitting the words out as he puffed up. "I was created centuries ago by your ancestors in Chichen Itza, the true home of the codices."

"Oh, very impressive." Hugh started pacing on his side of the codex. Jesus and his two companions didn't move.

"Why are you here so early?" Abilio asked.

"I was waiting for someone to bring that up!" Hugh said, a maniacal smile on his face. "You see, I called our dear mother last night, asking for news about my poor brother, who thought suicide was the answer in Paris."

"I didn't mean to—" Jesus said.

"You cut your own wrists! And, you would've been charged with theft in Paris if anyone but me discovered you with the codex. I saved you from rotting in a French jail."

Jesus glared at his twin.

"And she said that Abilio was on his way to Mexico City. And I thought to myself, 'That's odd. He's coming here and didn't say anything to me?' Then, I called the hospital, to see if my twin brother knew anything about Abilio's trip, and I found out that he wasn't there!

"And so I said to myself, 'Hugh, why would they come to Mexico City and not tell you?

"'But wait! Didn't Jesus try to steal the Paris Codex, and

couldn't he come for the Maya Codex of Mexico too?' And so, I spent the night watching the cameras."

"You stayed up all night?" Abilio asked.

Hugh reached into the front pocket of his messenger bag, withdrew a bottle of pills, and shook it. "Caffeine pills. Couldn't have gotten through college without them." He put the pills back into his bag. "Now, what I want to know is, how'd you do it in Dresden and Madrid and Paris without anyone seeing a big purple version of you?"

Jesus didn't bother explaining how his shadow hadn't been strong enough for such a robust display before two of the codices were back in Mexico. He set his jaw and kept his eyes on Hugh.

"Oh, you didn't think I knew about the other two, did you? To be honest, I really had no idea after Dresden. But did you know that your Madrid theft didn't go unnoticed? There are only a few of us who know—no need to make it public just yet. But then I realized there was one person who was in both Dresden and Madrid. You.

"Then, when you showed up in Paris, I knew it was only a matter of time. I must say, you didn't disappoint."

Jesus was tired of listening to his brother's rambling. He took off his backpack and gave it to Abilio. While focusing on his brother, he imagined his shadow form standing behind him.

Hugh's eyes grew wide with delight, and Jesus knew his shadow was there without turning around.

"If you won't give them to me, I'll just have to take them," Jesus said, setting his feet.

CHAPTER NINETEEN

"Ah, I was hoping you'd make this interesting," Hugh said. He lowered his head and held his straightened arms down at his side, palms open. His hands shook as he raised them, palms up, as if he was lifting them through thick honey.

A dull thud against the edge of the glass high overhead reverberated throughout the room. Another thud rang out, then another, all from different sides of the building, before the floodgates opened and the thuds became a continuous stream.

Jesus looked up; the windows were covered with a writhing black mass. Then, every window broke at once, and hundreds of bats streamed into the museum amid pieces of broken glass. Jesus and Abilio covered their heads. When Jesus looked again, the bats had streamed to his twin and became a swirling vortex around Hugh, obscuring his body.

"The bats belonged to the banished priest," Balam growled, his voice ringing clear above the din. "He was the first person who made shadow forms from the animals. Fighting them was the reason I was created in the first place."

"I thought you were a guide!" Jesus yelled, looking down at the purple jaguar.

Balam crouched; his tense muscles rippled.

Jesus looked back at his brother and saw the cloud split apart, the bats gathered at Hugh's outstretched hands. Standing behind Hugh was his dark purple shadow, a ten-foot-tall apparition in full Mayan war regalia. A black feathered headdress crowned its head, and a series of fused black necklaces covered its broad upper chest. A jaguar skull hung from a long necklace, resting over the shadow's belly, and the black loincloth it wore hung down to its knees.

Jesus looked back at his own shadow form and discovered it was also prepared for battle. Four broad bracelets—carved in the shape of jaguar heads—covered both forearms and upper arms. Instead of a headdress, his shadow wore a crown in the shape of a serpent, with the head of the snake protruding from its forehead.

There was a clear difference in size between the twins' shadow warriors. His own shadow was taller than both him and Hugh, but much smaller than Hugh's apparition. In addition to the difference in height, Hugh's shadow also looked much stronger—the muscles on its upper back made its neck look short, almost nonexistent.

Hugh looked at Jesus and smiled.

"Did you think you were the only one who knew how to access the shadow realm?" Hugh yelled over the beating bat wings.

Jesus felt a small part of himself deflate. "How did you learn?"

"They told me," Hugh said, gesturing towards the moving clouds gathered at his outstretched hands. "You can't understand them, but I can. They told me all about the jaguar that sent them to Xibalba—" The Mayan underworld. He looked at Balam. "They aren't happy with you."

"I took care of them once; I'll do it again," Balam said with a snarl.

Hugh brought his hands together and performed a series of small, slow claps in front of his wicked grin. "We were hoping you'd say that." He raised his eyebrows, and the bats surged forward, making a beeline for Balam.

The shadow jaguar took two powerful strides forward and launched himself into the dark cloud.

A portion of the bat cloud peeled off from the encounter with Balam and surrounded the Maya Codex on display. The glass case covering the ancient document rose in the air, exposing the artifact. Then, the cloud of bats emitted an earsplitting screech as they surged back to the fight with the jaguar, and hundreds of pieces of glass fell to the ground.

Hugh and Jesus met each other's gaze before they ran forward to the exposed codex from opposite sides. Abilio took refuge behind the statue of a Mayan warrior.

"I'm not letting you take it!" both twins yelled at the same time. Their shadow forms met on the left side of the codex display—opposite of Balam and the bats on the right—grabbing each other's arms before twisting and turning in an initial measure of strength.

Jesus didn't think about how his shadow moved on its own, trusting that it was based on an instinct he couldn't access without diving deep into his subconscious. All he cared about was the codex and making sure Hugh didn't take it. Neither twin reached for the codex, instead focusing on each other.

Whenever Jesus moved left, Hugh went right, maintaining the same distance between them.

"You can't avoid me forever!" Jesus yelled.

"I don't need forever—I just need long enough for my warriors to beat yours."

Jesus looked at his shadow form, now behind him. His

smaller shadow was scrambling back to its feet while Hugh's shadow watched, as if Hugh's shadow was playing with the smaller attacker. Balam and the cloud of bats were approaching Abilio, Balam weaving away from the darkest part of the cloud while snapping stray bats in half with his powerful jaws.

"Once they're done with your pitiful excuses for magic, I'll turn them on you and walk away with the codex in hand."

Jesus felt a small knot in the pit of his stomach erupt. The feeling coursed through his veins and surged into every corner of his body. He couldn't contain the scream.

Hugh laughed. "So you actually care about something! It's about time," Hugh said. His eyes grew wide when he saw Jesus climb onto the display table.

Jesus, keeping his legs wide so that he straddled the codex, ran the length of the table. Hugh feinted left, then right, before going left, and Jesus launched himself from the table and tackled his twin brother without any regard for his bandaged hand.

The messenger bag Hugh carried skidded across the floor.

Both Jesus and Hugh scrambled for the Paris Codex. Hugh pulled Jesus's leg and got ahead, then Jesus tripped Hugh as he passed. They were both on the ground reaching for the messenger bag when Abilio ran past and scooped it up.

"Get him!" Hugh yelled.

Jesus didn't see both Hugh's shadow and the bats leave their respective fights and chase Abilio—all he cared about was hurting Hugh. He climbed on top of his twin, turning him over so that Hugh's face was towards the ceiling. Then, he brought down a flurry of punches on his twin, releasing all of his frustrations.

Hugh laughed the entire time.

"Jesus!" Abilio yelled.

Jesus paused his assault and looked for his cousin. Abilio

was running from both the bats and Hugh's shadow on the far side of the room, weaving between statues; Hugh's shadow knocked them over during its pursuit. He slid under the table and emerged on the other side, where Balam met him while running in the opposite direction and launched himself at Hugh's shadow.

With the bats still on his tail, Abilio rounded the right side of the display table and ran towards Jesus. Jesus's shadow strode towards him. Jesus stood up and set his feet.

Abilio ran past, and Jesus pulled his arm back. His shadow met him at the same time, and together they punched the cloud of bats, sending a shock wave of purple shadow energy radiating out from the point of contact.

Jesus flew across the room. His back hit the wall, he felt something crack, and he crumpled to the floor.

"Get up!" Abilio screamed, holding out a hand and helping Jesus back to his feet.

Jesus leapt back up and jumped in the air, feeling rejuvenated. Hugh had folded the codex on display during the brief break in the fight. The bats, scattered after the blow, coalesced behind Hugh, and Balam separated from Hugh's shadow and rejoined Jesus. Jesus's own shadow reemerged from Jesus, squatted down, and slapped his thighs while opening his mouth: a threat and a warning for Hugh and his entourage.

Hugh smiled. "You're going to regret that," he said, wiping blood from his mouth.

Jesus watched Hugh start forward, leaving the folded codex on the display table; his shadow and bats surged ahead of him. Jesus's shadow met Hugh's once more, and Balam went back to work on the shadow bats. Hugh and Jesus met in the middle.

Hugh wound up and swung a long, looping right hook at his twin. Jesus blocked the shot and punched Hugh in the stomach while turning. His twin doubled over and rushed him, pushing him back against the table. Jesus felt a sharp pain in his lower back as he bent backward. Hugh grabbed Jesus's shirt collar and held him in place while punching his face.

But Hugh had forgotten about Abilio. His cousin, left alone while the three battles raged in the exhibit hall, ran to the table and put the folded codex into the messenger bag. He considered running before he saw Jesus's situation. Instead, he climbed onto the table, ran forward, and drop-kicked Hugh right in the chest.

"Let's go!" Abilio screamed, grabbing Jesus.

Jesus saw the world come back into focus, shook his head, and stood up straight.

Hugh climbed back to his feet. He looked somewhere in the distance behind Jesus and smiled.

Jesus turned around. The two shadow warriors disengaged, and Balam strode backward away from the cloud of shadow bats.

"Santi?" Jesus asked. "What are you doing here?"

Santiago García, wearing a white linen suit, stepped over a broken statue and navigated his way through the debris.

"I could ask you the same thing," he said. "And a few other questions too, I might add. For one, why did you keep the codices a secret from me? Mexico's greatest treasure, back on our soil," he said, hugging a backpack.

Jesus's backpack. With the two codices inside.

"I must say, you know your brother well," Santi continued, addressing Hugh. "Isabella called me and said she thought he might have them; said something about a safety-deposit box. But they were in the house, just like you said."

Jesus looked at Balam. "You didn't sense them missing?"

"I can't from this far away—only when we're both inside the ring of cenotes."

Santi shook his head, as if emerging from his thoughts.

"Wait a minute, what's all this?" he said, as if just seeing the two shadow warriors, jaguar, and bats for the first time.

Hugh walked around the table, giving Jesus a wide berth, and approached the Merida museum's patrón. "The codices provide magic powers," Hugh said. "Lets us control our dark side."

"Our shadows," Jesus corrected.

"That's what Balam told you? No wonder yours is so weak—you haven't even embraced the truth."

"And what told you the truth? The bats?"

Hugh raised his eyebrows twice.

"You lost something in translation," Jesus said.

Hugh shook his head and laughed. "I don't translate the sounds they make—I understand them, on a deeper level than you could ever appreciate. Getting caught up on the specific words poses challenges I don't have to deal with. Have you ever tried explaining 'love'? Can't do it, right? With the bats, I don't bother translating what they communicate with me to any language I know—I just listen and absorb."

"There's two right here, can you teach me how to do it?" Santi said, tapping the backpack in his hand.

"Do you have any Mayan blood?" Jesus called out.

"No," Santi said with disdain.

"Then you can't do it," Jesus said. His shadow stood next to him and crossed its arms.

"What are you talking about?"

Hugh put an arm on Santi's shoulder.

"He's right—only Mayan descendants can control the magic."

Santi looked like a petulant child just told no. It was a cross between holding his breath until his face turned red and the mask of disbelief, sprinkled with a hint of disgust at the upended power dynamics.

Jesus delighted in his boss being told no for once in his privileged life.

"Why is your shadow so much smaller than his?" Santi sneered, looking at Jesus.

"It won't be for much longer!" Abilio countered. "Here, take these!" he said, handing the messenger bag with the Maya Codex of Mexico and the Paris Codex inside to Jesus.

Jesus took the bag, expecting the power from holding two codices would give him the needed boost to match Hugh's firepower. He looked at his shadow . . .

Nothing. No change whatsoever.

Both Santi and Hugh laughed.

"We don't need it," Balam growled. "Ask the bats. This has already happened before, and will happen again. Time goes in circles, just like the calendar—the banished priest thought he was more powerful too."

"Oh, and what happened next?" Hugh said with mock fear.

"We killed him."

CHAPTER TWENTY

BALAM GROWLED AND TOOK OFF, bounding across the room.

"Wait!" Jesus said, holding an arm out.

The shadow jaguar skidded to a stop halfway to the bats swirling above Hugh and Santi. He started pacing left and right, his eyes never leaving his prey.

"You're not really going to kill him, are you?" Jesus said.

Hugh and Santi looked at each other, then laughed. "You're getting soft on me, brother. I'd like to see him try," Hugh said. Behind him, his shadow bent its knees and swayed side to side while staring at Balam, like a cobra in a trance.

"Mom would kill me," Jesus said.

"I can see that," Santi chimed in. "She's got some temper."

Hugh looked at Santi. "You've met our mom?"

"She was at the house when I took the codices." He lifted an arm and showed it to Hugh. "Scratched me pretty good."

"I swear, if you touched a hair on her head . . ." Jesus said. A display on the wall gave way, and a ceramic bowl came crashing to the floor, making everyone jump.

"You didn't do anything to her, did you?" Hugh asked.

"No, no, I just pushed her onto the bed. It was her own fault she fell off."

Hugh grabbed Santi by the collar.

"She's all right though, right?"

"Yes! She's fine. She sat up and stared at me as I walked out."

Hugh let go of Santi and smoothed the front of his shirt. "She better be."

"You're a coward!" Jesus said. He regretted stopping Balam.

"It was just her arm—she'll be fine," Santi said.

Hugh looked at Jesus with a questioning stare. "Why do you care? It's not like you're the one paying for any hospital bills."

Balam looked back at Jesus.

Jesus could feel Abilio's eyes on him.

Another time he couldn't protect his mom. But that didn't mean there wouldn't be any consequences.

Jesus met Balam's gaze and nodded. The shadow jaguar lowered his head and turned around. Then, Jesus sent his shadow running forward.

Hugh, realizing Jesus was sending his warriors back into battle, responded by sending his own shadow ahead of him, followed by the cloud of shadow bats.

Santi's eyes grew wide as Hugh's shadow shoved him aside and strode towards Balam.

The shadows clashed once more—Balam against the bats, and the twins' shadows against each other.

Jesus was about to run forward and attack Santi—through Hugh, if he had to—when he felt Abilio grab his arm.

"Wait," Abilio said.

"Why?" Jesus roared.

Abilio gestured towards the fight with his chin. Already, Balam was running in circles while the bats rained down from above, and Hugh's shadow warrior looked like it was playing with Jesus's all over again. And, behind it all, Hugh smiled with smug satisfaction.

"They'll turn on us next unless your team can work together," Abilio said.

Jesus pulled his arm away from Abilio's grasp with more force than intended. Then, when he realized his cousin was right, he thought about how the fighters from the shadow realm could help each other.

First, he sent Balam running away from the bats, charging towards the two shadow warriors engaged in combat. Then, he imagined Balam leaping into the air and launching his powerful jaws at the throat of Hugh's shadow.

So the bats wouldn't interfere, Jesus had his shadow stand up and clap in front of the bat cloud. It sent a shock wave through the bats, scattering them outward.

Hugh's shadow got two hands on Balam's chest and shoved him away. The jaguar landed on all fours next to Jesus's shadow warrior and skidded to a stop.

Jesus met Hugh's gaze and raised his eyebrows. The game was on.

Balam bounded back towards the bats with Hugh's shadow in pursuit. Jesus's shadow stepped forward as if he was going to attack Hugh's shadow. At the last moment, Jesus's shadow crouched down. Balam launched himself off the back of Jesus's shadow, and Hugh's shadow caught a shoulder right in the stomach, courtesy of Jesus's warrior. The shadow warriors fell to the ground in a heap while Balam spread all four legs wide and tore through the cloud of bats.

"Work together!" Hugh shouted in rage.

Instead of pressing the advantage, Jesus had his team recollect themselves and prepare for another strike. He imagined his shadow grabbing Balam by the tail and spinning the jaguar around so they could keep their opponents at a distance.

"That's a bit much," Balam yelled.

"Fine, fine," Jesus said.

Hugh's warrior surged forward from the right, and the bats attacked from the left. Without knowing why, Jesus imagined his shadow warrior dropping onto all fours. Balam crouched, waiting for the bats.

Jesus's warrior turned, grabbed Balam's tail, and pulled with all its might. The purple jaguar went flying backward, skidding on the tile floor, and ended up behind Hugh's warrior. Jesus's shadow launched into an upright stance and started swatting the bats with open palms while Balam leaped, attaching himself to the back of Hugh's warrior.

Jesus looked at Abilio. "Think you can take Santi?"

Abilio puffed up his cheeks and exhaled. "I'm not exactly a fighter . . ." He hurried his words when he saw the look on Jesus's face. "But I'll try."

"Let's do this," Jesus said. Together with his cousin, they ran around the table and between the occupied shadow fighters on their way to Hugh and Santi.

Santi, when he saw the pair coming, handed Hugh the backpack. Hugh slung it over his shoulders and tightened the straps.

Jesus ran full speed into his twin and tackled him to the floor. Abilio, when he was close to Santi, got cold feet.

"Look, I don't really know what I expected from all of this," Abilio said. "I'm too pretty to get hit."

Santi looked at Abilio, then at the messenger bag slung over his shoulder, and stepped towards him. Abilio ran away.

"I'm going to keep these safe!" Abilio yelled to Jesus, referring to the codices, while he weaved among the destruction.

"Get back here!" Santi snarled.

Jesus didn't hear his cousin. He saw red, furious at Hugh for getting Santi involved and putting their mother at risk. They rolled around on the floor, throwing the occasional punch, elbow, or knee, with neither brother getting the upper hand. Somehow, Jesus ended up on his back with his feet pressed against Hugh's chest, and he extended his legs as hard as he could.

Hugh went flying through the air. Both brothers got a sense of what a fall could mean for the codices at the same instant, and Hugh twisted in midair so he wouldn't crush the ancient documents.

The shadow fighters were breaking everything that had survived the initial destruction while they fought.

Abilio screamed across the room. Santi was on top of him, sitting on his chest while the young man squirmed. The messenger bag with the two codices was on the ground next to them, the strap still slung around Abilio's shoulders.

"Get off of me!" Abilio yelled.

Santi raised his arm and slapped Abilio across the face with an open hand.

The sound of the slap hurt Jesus worse than any physical pain ever had. Everything about the situation, from the shadow fighters to the codices, left his mind, and just one desire remained: keeping Abilio safe. He ran towards Abilio and Santi, watching as Santi raised his arm once again despite Abilio not fighting back. He passed his shadow slapping the bats . . .

And flew sideways when Hugh tackled him to the ground. Jesus watched in horror as Santi raised his arm and struck Abilio yet again, squirming while Hugh held him fast with arms around his midsection.

Jesus put an arm around Hugh's neck and squeezed.

Hugh pushed his knees into the ground and pulled his body away, but Jesus didn't relent.

Abilio turned his reddened face to the side and looked at Jesus. He reached an arm out and opened the messenger bag's flap. "Summon them to you," he said.

Jesus didn't hear his cousin's words over the noise of the fighting but understood the message.

He looked at the codices, picturing the ancient pages and the Mayan script written on them, letting them overtake his awareness.

Hugh struggled in the headlock.

Then, he imagined his shadow taking the codices from the bag . . .

All of a sudden, Jesus hit a mental block. He couldn't imagine his shadow doing anything, no matter how hard he tried. Then, he realized what was wrong: his shadow was already in the physical realm. There was no entity in the shadow realm that he could manipulate.

Jesus rearranged his position so that he could look at his shadow fighting the bats. Balam battled Hugh's warrior past them.

The shift in their bodies gave Hugh the space he needed. He pulled his head out of Jesus's grasp and took in large gulps of air.

Jesus made a split-second decision—he just hoped it would work.

He focused on the bats, imagining them attacking him instead of his shadow. Since there was no way he could pay attention to a single animal, he stared at the moving cloud, watching the shape transform as it attacked his shadow warrior. He imagined his shadow lying down on the ground in the exact same position he was in, then bringing the bats to him through the shadow realm.

With any luck, they'd keep attacking his physical form, freeing up his shadow.

He focused on the bats once more, giving over his awareness to the dark purple cloud.

The next thing he knew, they were on top of him. They

dove down, beating him with their small wings, scratching his skin with sharp claws. He covered his face, worried about his eyes.

A shadow jaguar couldn't hold Hugh's shadow in place, but another warrior could. Jesus had his shadow form run across the room and tackle Hugh's, pinning the warrior on the ground. Then, Balam started running towards Abilio.

Meanwhile, Hugh was yelling at the bats. "No, don't attack him! He can't do anything!"

The bats didn't listen, caught in their bloodlust.

Balam launched himself at Santi. The force of the impact knocked the patrón sideways; he hit his head and tumbled to the ground, unconscious.

Then, Balam turned on Hugh. By now, the twin had command of the bats, and he had sent them back to his own shadow, hoping they could team up on Jesus's shadow warrior. He didn't see the shadow jaguar bound across the room, launch himself in the air, and, using his head as a battering ram, strike Hugh behind the ear.

Hugh collapsed onto the ground in a heap. The bat cloud dissipated, no longer enslaved, and the individual animals went flying out of the broken windows in search of somewhere they could sleep the day away. Hugh's shadow warrior disappeared, leaving Jesus's warrior clutching thin air.

Jesus rushed over to Abilio's side. He kneeled down and lifted his head.

His cousin's cheeks were bright red, and he had a cut over his right eye. Snot and tears covered his cheeks.

"Are you all right?" Jesus said. As he watched, Abilio's cut started getting smaller, then disappeared. His cheeks' normal color returned, and he sat up.

"I'm fine," Abilio said.

"You just—you just—" Jesus stammered.

"I just what?" Abilio said, wiping his face with his shirt.

"You just healed yourself," Balam said, the pride evident in his voice.

"I did?" Abilio said, touching his eye. He looked up while feeling his face, focusing on his senses.

"You can heal with just a touch," Balam explained.

Abilio looked at Jesus and noticed the scratches on his neck and arms, and the bruises on his face from Hugh's elbows. He looked at his hand, then grabbed Jesus's wrist.

All of Jesus's injuries went away. What was more, both Balam and Jesus's shadow warrior appeared rejuvenated, as if they had never fought at all.

Jesus helped Abilio to his feet, and together they walked over to the knocked-out Hugh. Jesus reached down and took the backpack from his twin.

"Did you really kill the banished priest?" Abilio asked Balam.

"We sacrificed him to the thunder god, Chaac," Balam said.

Abilio looked horrified.

"Things were different back then. Being sacrificed was a great honor; it was the banished priest's last request."

"Well, you didn't mention that," Abilio said.

"Wouldn't have had the same effect," Balam replied.

"So we have all four codices now," Jesus said, looking at the destruction around him. There wasn't a single exhibit left intact. Even most of the furniture was destroyed.

"Did you want to . . ." Jesus said to Abilio, pointing to Hugh.

"Heal him? After all that? No thanks, let's just get out of here," Abilio said. He looked down at the skin on his hands and opened the messenger bag slung over his shoulder. "I wonder if Hugh has any lotion in this bag—I know you don't have any in that backpack."

CHAPTER TWENTY-ONE

"Ok, everyone, you have thirty minutes before the bus takes off again. Don't be late!" barked the bus driver, a heavyset man sporting a days-old beard, as he trudged off of the bus.

Watching the bus driver through the window, Jesus saw him shuffle to the rest stop's main building like the bathroom break couldn't have come soon enough.

Jesus shifted the messenger bag containing all four codices on his lap and slung the strap over one shoulder. Abilio zipped up the backpack with Balam inside, back in house cat form, and put it onto his back. The two of them followed their fellow passengers off the bus. Once outside, they stretched—Abilio reaching for the sky and leaning back, Jesus twisting and cracking his lower back.

"That wasn't so bad," Abilio said, a repeat of his statement when they had gotten off of the bus in Mexico City.

"That's because you fell asleep as soon as we got on," Jesus replied.

The sun was on its way down in the sky. The rest stop was packed, with a handful of other buses both parked and fueling up at the pumps, along with dozens of cars.

"Let's get something to eat," Jesus said.

Abilio reached into his pocket and withdrew his wallet. He showed it, empty, to Jesus. "I'm all out of cash . . ." he said.

Jesus squinted and shook his head. "I'll pay."

Abilio smiled. "Then let's get something to eat!"

They walked into the large stone building the bus driver had disappeared into moments before. The bathrooms were on their right, an open space in the wall that diverted to the left and right for men and women. On their left was a gift shop selling blankets, souvenirs, and gifts. The pair continued through the short hall and emerged into an open space filled with circular metal tables and simple metal chairs. A restaurant on the far wall sold everything from soup and sandwiches to fruit and candy. There were two other entrances to the space, one on the left wall and the other ahead of them, and next to these were refrigerators filled with various types of soda and specialty bottled beverages.

Jesus and Abilio ordered two chicken sandwiches. With their food in hand, they sat down at one of the tables near the gift shop. The bus driver, having emerged from the bathroom, sat down at a nearby table with a soda and a basic sandwich on white bread he had brought from home. Jesus kept the messenger bag on his lap, but Abilio set the backpack down on the floor, unzipping the top so Balam could get some air.

A nearby diner saw the cat's head poke out of the bag and turned away.

"What's wrong?" Abilio said to Jesus with a mouthful of food.

Jesus looked up from his sandwich. "Huh?"

"I said, 'What's wrong?' You've been pretty quiet since we left Mexico City."

"Well, you were asleep for most of it," Jesus replied.

Abilio shrugged and took another bite.

Jesus sighed. "I can't stop thinking about what Santi said, how Isabella told him the codices might be in a safety-deposit box. I didn't think she'd say anything to him."

"Why wouldn't she? He's the one who pays for everything at the museum," Abilio said through a mouthful of food.

"I don't know. I thought we were friends." When Abilio didn't say anything, Jesus added that he knew that she was upset about him going to Paris. "But I didn't think she'd turn around and talk to Santi about me."

"Well, she wasn't wrong—you did have the codices. Just not where she thought."

"It was probably hard for her too," Balam said.

"Shhh," Jesus said, looking around. None of the other diners paid them any attention, but if they had, they would have wondered about the third voice. The last thing Jesus needed was everyone knowing he traveled with a talking cat.

"He's right," Abilio said. "She's in charge of a museum. Knowing there are priceless artifacts nearby, she probably felt like she had to do something."

Jesus nodded and took a bite of his sandwich. Looking for a distraction, he took out his phone. There were dozens of missed calls from both Santi and Hugh, one from Isabella, and one from his mother. Beatriz had even left a voicemail.

"Jesus. Give me a call when you get this. Hugh's looking for you, and he's got me worried."

"Who was it?" Abilio said when Jesus lowered the phone, before taking a sip of his Coca-Cola.

"Mom. She said Hugh's looking for me."

"Of course he is. You going to call her back?"

"After we eat; just to let her know we're safe."

Jesus set his phone down and took a bite of his sandwich.

A disheveled man stumbled into the dining area, muttering to himself. Parts of his hair stuck to his head, and other tufts jutted out at odd angles, giving him the appearance of a man with horns. Jesus watched the workers go on high alert as soon as they noticed the man, anticipating the worst.

The man approached the tables near the entrance, holding his hands out for whatever the diners could spare. The older women he first approached ignored him, pretending he didn't exist. The second table he visited was a young family, a man and a woman with two small children. He paused his incoherent muttering long enough to say some words—Jesus couldn't hear exactly what—and one of the toddlers started crying. The father, a burly man, stood up in a rage and shoved the beggar to the ground.

Nobody helped him up.

The man stayed down for a few moments, staring at the ceiling as if he had given up. Then, as he rolled over and sat up, a stream of men wearing Mexican army uniforms walked into the rest stop. The one in front, the man with the most badges and medals, approached the beggar and poked him with the toe of his black boot.

"What are you doing on the floor. Get up," the army officer said.

"He pushed me down," the beggar said, pointing to the young father.

The father launched into a tirade about how he just wanted to eat a decent meal with his family and how they were tired from their trip and still had half a day to go. The officer looked down his nose at the beggar, who was muttering to himself again.

"And he made my boy cry," the father added, finishing his rant.

"Disturbing the peace, huh?" the army officer said. He signaled to two of his men then pointed at the beggar. "Get him out of here."

The two men lifted the beggar, took him to the closest entrance, and threw him on the concrete sidewalk outside before following him through the doors.

Jesus and the officer locked eyes before Jesus looked away and finished the last of his sandwich. "Let's get out of here," he said to Abilio.

They went back out the entrance near the buses, the one opposite where the beggar was thrown out.

"We've still got fifteen minutes before the bus leaves," Abilio said, looking at his phone. "Why don't we let Balam walk around a bit."

"Agreed," a muffled voice said from the backpack hanging from Abilio's shoulders.

Jesus nodded. "Not here though." He led them away from the building, and they walked along the trees on the opposite side of the road. There was a well-worn path into the brush; they followed it through the foliage and found a clearing.

"Set a timer," Jesus told Abilio.

Abilio nodded and set one on his phone before putting the backpack on the ground and unzipping it all the way. Balam bounded out, transforming back into the purple shadow jaguar in midair, while Jesus made a call.

"Mom?"

"Yes, I'm fine."

"He's with me too, I'm looking right at him."

Jesus held out the phone.

"We're safe!" Abilio shouted.

"Ok, I'll tell him."

Jesus hung up the phone and told Abilio that Beatriz said to make sure he brushes his teeth.

Abilio sighed and shook his head. "I forgot one time, years ago, and she still says that," he said.

Jesus laughed.

"Can you feel it?" Balam said, walking in a slow circle, the tip of his thick tail just ahead of his face. "All four codices. It's like feeling the sun's warmth, but deeper."

Jesus walked around in the clearing, beneath the sun, feeling the heat on his skin while he searched for the extra power. He thought he could sense it, but he wasn't sure, so he looked for something he could teleport using his powers. On one side of the clearing was a large slab of metal leaning against a tree, with a dirt path emerging from one side.

He guessed the metal would be heavy and awkward—the perfect test. Focusing on the metal, his shadow was on the verge of emerging . . .

"Stop," Balam whispered. Jesus looked at the cat and saw he was small again. Balam stared in the direction of the rest stop, and both Jesus and Abilio followed his gaze.

A twig cracked, then the beggar stumbled into the clearing. His face was bruised, his nose was bleeding, and he walked with a noticeable limp. He looked through the three people in his clearing as if they weren't there, muttered something about the president searching for him, then struggled towards the piece of metal Jesus almost teleported.

"They got you good," Abilio said, his voice carrying a hint of sadness.

"Huh?" the beggar said, seeing the others for the first time.

Jesus remembered when Abilio had gotten beat up by some of the local boys for being different. Ever since then, his cousin had made sure he stayed in well-lit areas at night when he wasn't working at the fruit stand.

The more Jesus thought about it, the more he realized Abilio healed faster than expected, even all those years ago, before the codices came back to Mexico.

Abilio walked towards the beggar. "I can help," he said.

The beggar flinched and cowered, as if Abilio was another attacker.

"It's all right," Abilio soothed. He lowered his head so he could better see the beggar's face.

The scared man turned his head enough so he could see Abilio. Then, transfixed, he stood up straight and looked him in the eye.

Jesus had seen his cousin the clown and his cousin the friend, but he had never seen his cousin the healer. His pride surged, catching in his throat.

"Will you let me help?" Abilio asked.

The man gave Abilio a slight nod.

"Hold out your hands," Abilio said, holding out his own.

Jesus realized the man had been clutching one hand close the entire time. As he held them out, it became clear why: the fingers on the left hand were bent at odd angles.

"It's okay," Abilio said when the man hesitated. "Just rest your hands on mine. I'll take care of the rest."

The man took a breath and exhaled. He laid his hands on Abilio's upturned palms, and Abilio wrapped his thumbs around them.

"Look at me," Abilio said, smiling.

The man stared at Abilio's face, and Jesus watched the bruises disappear. The broken fingers twisted back to normal, and the man put weight back on his right leg.

Abilio smiled, and the man's eyes grew wide.

"It's so . . . quiet," the man whispered.

Jesus furrowed his brow. From the clearing, they could hear the cars pulling into the rest stop, people shouting at each other, and birds in the trees around them. Plenty of noise.

"The voices went away," the man whispered. Then, when the truth sunk in, he shouted. "The voices went away!"

He pulled his hands away from Abilio and started dancing.

"What did you do to me?" he asked Abilio. His eyes grew wide. "Magia," he whispered.

Abilio held a finger up to his lips. "My grandmother taught me."

The man looked at Abilio with wide eyes before collapsing onto the ground and wrapping his arms around Abilio's ankles. "Thank you, thank you, thank you! I thought I was hearing the satellites!"

Abilio's phone alarm went off. He pulled it out of his pocket and held it up to Jesus.

"Time to go," he said. Balam hopped back into the back-pack, and, together with Jesus, they left the beggar behind as he promised a new, changed life.

"Imagine how many people you could help with your powers," Jesus said, clapping Abilio on the back as they emerged from the trees.

"Imagine how many people we will help, once there are more healers than just me."

CHAPTER TWENTY-TWO

THE BUS PASSED by a sign with a symbolic representation of Chichen Itza's main pyramid, the Temple of Kukulcán, above an arrow pointing straight ahead. On each side of the road, small hotels, restaurants, and stores all played on the theme of the ancient Mayan city of Chichen Itza: Hotel Chichen Itza, Souvenirs Chichen Itza, and Puerto Chichen. There was even a restaurant called Balam House, the Mayan word for jaguar.

Jesus had assumed he would be rejuvenated on their approach, ready for the culmination of two consecutive long journeys by bus and weeks of international travel. Instead, he felt tired. It was nine in the morning, just a half hour before the equinox, when the codices needed to be at the main pyramid.

The bus turned onto the narrow access road, the final leg of their trip. Soon, the Mayan magic would be back with his people. He could figure out what came next after completing his quest.

He nudged Abilio. "Wake up; we're almost there."

Abilio rubbed the sleep from his eyes and looked out through the bus's windshield.

"What's going on?" he said.

Jesus leaned over and followed his cousin's gaze. Ahead of them, people were running away from the site's entrance, waving away the incoming vehicles. A steady stream of cars flowed in the opposite direction, the drivers all honking and waving the bus back through open windows.

The bus driver kept going despite the warnings—there wasn't enough room to turn around.

By the time the bus got to the parking lot, they were moving forward at a crawl because of the fleeing visitors. It wasn't just tourists; Jesus also saw people fleeing from the entrance carrying crates and blankets filled with souvenirs. The people who showed up each day when the ancient site opened in the morning, so they could set up their tables along the walkways and sell everything from magnets to carved masks to the tourists, also hurried away from the ancient city.

Why would they abandon their posts, on what should be one of the busiest days of the year?

Static crackled through the overhead speaker as the bus driver turned on the microphone. "I'm turning us around. We can figure out what's going on back on the main road."

Abilio spoke up before Jesus could find his voice. "Drop us off!" he said.

An older female passenger looked at the two of them. "Are you crazy? Who knows what's going on?" she said with a sternness uncharacteristic for a stranger.

Jesus looked at her. She could have been his grandmother, or a great aunt. "You know what's crazy? Going from Merida to Mexico City, then Mexico City to here, in two days."

"We've traveled a long way to get here too, but it isn't safe," she said, her tone softening. "Look, everyone's running away."

"We have to do this," Jesus said to the woman. Then, to the bus driver, he yelled, "Drop us off here if you don't want to get any closer!"

The bus driver slowed down the bus, and the door opened with a hiss. Everyone inside the vehicle stared at Jesus and Abilio as they disembarked with their bags in tow. The door closed as soon as they got off, and the bus driver put the vehicle back into gear, despite the fact that it couldn't move much because of the traffic.

"What's going on?" Jesus asked a passing merchant rolling three crates on a handcart.

"Shots fired inside the park. It's too early for this," she said, shaking her head and hurrying away.

Abilio let Balam out of his backpack and put the bag back on his shoulders, empty. Then, the three of them ran up the steps to the entrance to the complex.

There are many structures at Chichen Itza; the Temple of Kukulcán is the most famous, and the picture of the pyramid is what pops up on a Google search. But there are also the Temple of the Warriors and the Great Ball Court, in addition to many other ancillary buildings in various states of preservation. To see any of these, visitors have to pass through the entrance station, where guards make sure everyone pays the cost of admission. There is a different price for Mexican citizens; most of the money made comes from international visitors brought by the busload from Cancun. Inside the entrance station are a restaurant, a souvenir shop, several food vendors, and a bathroom.

When Jesus, Abilio, and Balam got to the official entrance, they were met by a wall of guards turning everyone back and helping people exit the site. One of the guards looked at them, eyed the cat at their feet with suspicion, and waved them away.

There were rumors of a few secret entrances through the surrounding jungle, ones that locals knew about and frequented. The guards turned a blind eye in exchange for kickbacks every now and then, and it was how most of the people who sold trinkets to tourists along the footpaths got into the site;

their meager profits would take a hit if they had to pay the entrance fee every day. Plus, at the end of the day, most of the vendors were of Mayan descent, and everyone, even the guards, agreed that they had the right to profit off the visitors to the site their ancestors built.

Jesus just didn't know where any of the secret entrances were.

Turned away from the main entrance, Jesus and Abilio went back down the stairs and looked around.

"There's got to be another way in around here somewhere; we only have twenty minutes. Left or right?" Jesus asked Abilio.

His cousin looked both ways. Then, he spotted a young man carrying a large stack of blankets on his head, marching away. He wore tight black pants, a ring on his pinky finger, and a silver earring that dangled from his ear. "Hey!" Abilio said, running up to the man. "What's another way in?"

The young man looked around then gestured with his chin to the left of the main entrance. "Back there," he said. "Be careful though, they're shooting." He looked at Jesus with curiosity before shaking his head and walking away.

"Let's go," Abilio said.

Balam led the way through the undergrowth. He weaved in and out of the brush while Jesus and Abilio climbed over and under vines, walked around large trees, and contended with pokes from stiff leaves and thorns. The plant growth because of the codices made the foliage more dense as they walked, slowing their progress.

Within minutes, Jesus and Abilio saw more people streaming away from Chichen Itza through the trees, carrying the goods they'd come to sell, and they turned onto the path with fifteen minutes left before the spring equinox, when the serpent shadow would appear on the Temple of Kukulcán.

They climbed over a neglected stone wall and emerged into

the manicured lawns that designated the preserved area of Chichen Itza. Behind them, the jungle creeped forward, the plant growth spurred on by the codices.

Jesus looked at his watch: 9:21. Just over ten minutes until the sun crossed the celestial equator.

Ahead of them was a massive stone wall. Jesus guessed where they were, but it wasn't until they hurried forward and saw the top of the Temple of Kukulcán ahead on their right and the parallel twin wall that he knew for sure that they had emerged from the jungle behind the Great Ball Court.

The ancient Maya played a high-stakes game with a hard rubber ball, a combination of soccer and basketball. Instead of using hands and feet, athletes used the hips, thighs, and upper arms while trying to get the ball through a hoop high in the air. Games could last hours, and the captain of the winning team was given the honor of being sacrificed to Chaac, the rain god; their death would bring their people renewed life.

The Great Ball Court at Chichen Itza was the largest ball court ever built, about the size of one and a half soccer fields. There were two parallel stone walls, each the height of four men stacked on top of each other, with a hoop in the center of each wall near the top. The captain stood on a raised platform at the bottom of the stone walls, barking orders to his team in hopes that they would be the ones who got the rubber ball through their hoop first.

Below the raised platforms were well-preserved carved panels of ball players, showing their traditional athletic gear: sandals, protective gear on the areas where they struck the ball, and feathered headdresses. Jesus remembered coming here as a kid and wondering if the person who had carved the images did so with blood dripping down the surface from a recent sacrificial decapitation.

A single gunshot and distant shouting pulled Jesus from his

memory. They were running out of time. Of all the days for a gunman to take over Chichen Itza, it had to be the one day, at the one time, he needed to be at the main temple.

Jesus led the way around the remains of a smaller building and turned to see the front face of the Temple of Kukulcán through the trees on the side of the footpath.

There wasn't just a single gunman. Instead, there was a group of people dressed in all black, standing with the air of military members. In front of them, obscured by their bodies, were a handful of people wearing normal clothes.

Hostages.

Jesus didn't understand. Who were these people? He looked down at his phone. Nine minutes left.

"Balam, do you think you can distract them?"

Balam peered out through the thickening growth. "No better than you can. Send your shadow with me and we can try to scare them off."

Jesus was about to focus on his shadow when one of the people dressed in black turned around. It was a woman, with short black hair and a sharp face. He got a sense of recognition that he couldn't shake.

Where had he seen her?

She turned back to the center as one of the hostages approached. The man put a hand on her shoulder with familiarity; when she let him pass her position so that he could get a better view of the temple from farther away, Jesus saw that he was wearing a clean white suit with a bright red button-down shirt and a matching red pocket square.

Santiago García.

The woman? His guard, the same one that was with him in the museum in Merida.

The people behind the guards weren't hostages, they were

the ones taking Chichen Itza for themselves! And if Santi was there . . .

Another one of the guards moved, and Jesus saw Hugh.

Jesus looked at his phone and watched another minute tick away. He took a deep breath and embraced Abilio.

"Stay here," he whispered.

"What do you mean?" Abilio shook his head as the truth dawned on him. He pulled away but stayed at arm's reach. "No, no, I'm coming with you!"

"No, it's too dangerous."

"But what if you get hurt? I need to be there to heal you!"

"Give me at least through the equinox. Can you do that for me?"

Abilio bit his lip.

"Abilio," Jesus said in a loud whisper. "Can you give me through the equinox?"

Abilio nodded.

Without delay, Jesus called forth his shadow form. It disappeared from the ground, and he knew it was behind him when Abilio's eyes grew wide. Something about Abilio's sheer awe and lack of words made him curious.

He turned around and saw that his shadow was as tall as Hugh's had been, and just as muscular. What's more, the deep purple stood out against the green of the ever-growing plants around them, making it seem solid and real. The edges, instead of being blurry, shone gold.

Jesus looked down at Balam, who was looking up at him.

"Whatever happens out there, you've made your ancestors proud," Balam said.

"Are you coming with me?" Jesus asked.

"I wouldn't miss it for the world."

Together with Balam, Jesus emerged from the undergrowth and started walking towards the main face of the Temple of

Kukulcán through the wide-open, well-tended lawn, his shadow walking behind them.

Santi's guards all aimed their weapons at him, and Jesus stopped walking. The last of the people wearing civilian clothes turned around, and he saw that Isabella was with Santi and Hugh as well.

"Oh, so it's that kind of party?" Hugh yelled, holding out his arms. All of a sudden, a sea of bats flew from behind the temple, obscuring the area behind him. They parted a moment later, and Hugh's shadow stood behind him, arms open, mimicking Hugh, with a cloud of bats swirling around each hand.

Jesus swallowed. It was him and Balam against a small army, and he had a little more than five minutes left.

CHAPTER TWENTY-THREE

"JUST GIVE us the codices and nobody gets hurt," Santi shouted.

Jesus clutched the messenger bag at his side. "I can't do that."

Balam started pacing in front of Jesus, like a hunting dog waiting for the command.

Hugh walked past the line of guards, approaching Jesus. He stopped a few paces past their raised weapons, still dozens of paces away from his twin. His shadow and the bats stayed where they were.

"Now that all four codices are back in Mexico, why don't we tell the world that what belongs to us is finally home?" Hugh said.

"I told you, it's bigger than that," Jesus said, glaring at his brother.

"Bigger? What's bigger than history? Than owning history? Don't you have any Mexican pride?"

"We can bring back magic for the Maya."

"The Maya," Hugh scoffed. "They had magic before, and what did they do with it? Nothing. They let a bunch of Spaniards walk into their homes and destroy their culture. It's better off with us, with me. At least we'll know what to do with it!"

"Don't you have any Mayan pride? Or did you forget where you came from?"

Hugh rolled his eyes and started pacing. "How could I forget? I'm reminded of it every time I look in the mirror!"

"You can't outrun what you are," Jesus mouthed.

His twin understood despite the lack of sound. "I'm doing the best I can," a frustrated Hugh snapped.

In that moment, for the first time, Jesus felt sorry for his twin. Despite his accomplishments, education, and position, Hugh still hadn't accepted who he was.

"Look, Santi's serious about getting these codices into the museums. He's already talking about how mad Dresden, Madrid, and Paris will be!" Hugh lowered his voice. "I don't think he cares if you end up dead."

Jesus looked at Santi's security detail, all aiming their weapons at him. "No kidding."

Santi, upon seeing Jesus inspecting his mercenaries, stepped forward. "Look, just hand over the codices and we can all pretend this didn't happen. We can even give you a nice, easy job at the museum." He turned to Isabella. "Right?"

Isabella looked like she had been pulled from a dream. She blinked twice and nodded her head.

Jesus ignored Santi and turned his attention back to Hugh. "How did you even know I was headed here?" he asked.

Hugh pointed at Balam. "He said so, when I caught you stealing the codex from the anthropology museum."

"I never said that," Balam said in defiance.

"The codices' true home? Ring any bells?"

Balam bared his fangs, upset that Hugh was correct.

"Look, we can bring glory back to Mexico and our family.

Nobody else has powers yet; we can share the magic. Think about all the good we can do."

"Abilio has powers."

A flash of surprise passed over Hugh's face, but an instant later he had regained composure. "Then he can help us too!"

"You've never cared about our family before," Jesus said, taking a step forward. "You act like we're something you need to run away from and now, as soon as there's something you want, we're family again?"

Hugh's eyes narrowed.

"No, our family is every Maya who had their culture burned by the Spanish all those years ago."

Jesus took another step forward. Santi whispered something to the woman in charge of the mercenaries, and she fired a shot at Jesus's feet.

"Not another step, son," Santi said with a paternal air.

"I'm not your son!" Jesus roared.

Santi turned to Isabella. "Can you talk some sense into him?"

Isabella shrunk and took a small step forward. "You don't care about your well-being," she observed. "Or else you wouldn't have risked everything stealing the codices."

Jesus nodded in agreement.

"But think about the documents. Where are you going to put them? Are they going to be exposed to the elements? We need to keep them safe, and protected, in the museum. You talk about the Spanish burning all the Mayan books—are you willing to risk the last four remnants of Mayan writing that exist?"

Jesus realized Isabella had hit on something he hadn't considered. He knelt down next to Balam. "Where am I supposed to put the codices? Just at the chamber on top?"

Balam turned his bright yellow eyes away from Hugh and

looked at Jesus. "The codices are all we have left of our culture's foundation. Look at the temple and you'll see."

There, at the ground level, a faint purple rectangular shadow appeared. A door.

Hugh followed Jesus's gaze; the rest of his entourage also turned and saw.

"So that's where they go," Hugh said. "You think you can get through all of us?"

Jesus started when the sound of engines came roaring from the direction of the entrance. Because of the acoustics at Chichen Itza, the echoes reverberated off the walls, making it sound like there were many vehicles on their way.

There were.

A steady stream of troop transport vehicles stormed into the wide-open field around the Temple of Kukulcán. The grass was already longer because of the presence of the codices, and the tires created thick tracks as they sped towards the standoff.

Santi and his head pistolero walked towards the leading vehicle with their hands up. The rest of the mercenaries aimed their weapons at the ground.

"Veronica Chavez," the woman said, holding up her identification. "This gentleman has stolen government property," she said, pointing to Jesus.

An older troop, a short man with slicked-back black hair peppered with gray, stepped out of the passenger side of the lead vehicle and approached Santi and Veronica.

"There were reports of gunshots." He looked past the pair at Jesus, and his eyes grew wide when he saw Jesus's shadow warrior behind and the jaguar standing next to him, across from Hugh's shadow form.

"We had to clear the area. This man is a danger to the public."

"What the hell are those things?" the officer said.

"No time to explain. Can your men help us?" Hugh yelled.

The officer shook his head, clearing his momentary trance. "What did you say he had?"

"Government property—the four remaining Mayan codices in the world. He wants to sacrifice them at the Temple of Kukulcán. They'd be gone forever," Veronica said.

"How'd he get them?"

"He stole them, sir. From museums across the globe."

The officer thought for a moment. Then, with a wave, he sent some of his vehicles around the temple, leaving the other half with him. Within seconds, dozens of troops poured out of their vehicles and took aim at Jesus, adding to the forces already standing in his way.

Jesus took a deep breath. He felt the connection to his shadow form coursing through his body, the magic from the codices stronger than any stimulant. He wondered if he could teleport all of the guns away from the people aiming at him— maybe he could have before the reinforcements came, but he sensed that the new arrivals put the number beyond his capabilities.

What he needed was a distraction. He considered sending his shadow warrior and Balam ahead of him, forging a path, but Hugh had already proven he could handle both entities.

So it came down to a single question: How many could he take down with him? He wasn't going to give up without a fight. Plus, he wondered how much the codices really mattered to those standing in his way. Would they shoot him and put the codices at risk? A bullet could pierce them, he could fall on them or cover them in blood—whatever happened, the ancient documents would end up damaged.

He rearranged himself so that his left foot was in front of his right and bent at the hip, preparing for his mad dash. Balam crouched, ready. Jesus didn't have to look at his shadow warrior to know that it relished the chance for another crack at Hugh's.

"Hunahpu! What are you thinking?" The familiar voice came from Jesus's left, near the back corner of the Temple of the Warriors.

Jesus turned and saw Beatriz, followed by a sizable retinue of fellow Mayan elders. There for the spring equinox, just like every year.

And, like in years past, they'd taken one of the hidden paths so that they didn't have to pay in order to visit the site their ancestors built.

The elders marched their way through the shin-high grass and stood in a line between Jesus and Hugh.

"We were going to watch the equinox from the trees because of the shooting—we haven't missed an equinox yet and didn't intend to start today!" Beatriz said.

The other elders nodded.

"Can you imagine how surprised I was to see my two sons standing in front of the temple, one of them standing with the man who broke into my house!" A murmur broke out among the elders; they had heard about Beatriz's home intruder.

She leveled a stern gaze at Hugh. "You're right at the serpent's mouth; the gate to the underworld is open today."

Hugh looked at his shadow, then at Santi, and laughed. The pistoleros all joined in, and a few of the troops chuckled.

"You stand there with a magical warrior at your back and you still don't believe in the old ways," Beatriz said, shaking her head.

The codices started vibrating as the equinox approached. The messenger bag left Jesus's side, urging him forward. Jesus took a step.

"Don't come any closer!" Hugh said.

"Or what?" Beatriz countered. "You're going to kill all of us?"

The implied threat fortified the elders. They stood tall and linked arms.

Jesus reached forward and put a hand on Beatriz's shoulder. "Don't do this. Get everyone out of here; it's not safe."

A small purple mark, ringed in gold, appeared at the spot where Jesus touched Beatriz and started spreading. She took a deep breath when it reached her throat, and it spread down her body and to the other elders connected to her. As it raced down the line in both directions, the bond between the elders coalesced; they were stronger and more resolute.

"We're not going anywhere," Beatriz said, determined.

All at once, the line of elders took a step forward. Then another. All in unison and without any visible command.

"They're connected!" Santi yelled.

Jesus followed behind the wall.

For a moment, Hugh appeared unsure. Then, his rage overtook him and he sent his bats surging forward.

The cloud clashed with a wall in front of the elders, sending bright purple flashes from each point of impact.

"Ignore them, get Jesus!" Hugh yelled.

The bats rose high into the air, over the shield provided by the elders, and came streaming down on Jesus from overhead.

The instant before they hit him, his shadow warrior stuck a bent arm over Jesus, protecting him from the onslaught.

"Be careful with the codices!" Isabella yelled from beyond the tumult.

Through the elders, Jesus saw Hugh address Isabella. "If I can't have them, nobody will," he snarled. He turned and sent his shadow warrior forward.

Balam leaped over the elders and met Hugh's shadow head-on. They collapsed onto the grass, now grown to right below Jesus's knee.

The elders kept marching forward, with Jesus following behind. Jesus looked out at the guns still pointed in their direction and worried for his mother's safety.

"You don't have to do this!" he shouted behind her.

Beatriz turned around and approached her son. Her shadow form stayed in line, maintaining their unified front. She put her hands on his cheeks, looking into his eyes.

"There's nowhere else I'd rather be. You're my son."

"But Hugh's your son too."

Beatriz nodded with a sigh. "He is, but he's confused."

"Aren't you scared?" he blurted out. Worrying about his mother's fear made him realize his own.

"Terrified," Beatriz said with a smile. "But this is about more than just us, right?"

Jesus looked at the elders, at Hugh, at the army and Isabella and Santi. He even turned around and took another look at Abilio, watching from behind a tree.

"Right?" Beatriz repeated.

Jesus turned back to his mother and nodded. "Right."

From over Beatriz's shoulder, Jesus saw Veronica aim her rifle at Beatriz's back. She pulled the trigger, and the sound of the gunshot reverberated throughout Chichen Itza.

CHAPTER TWENTY-FOUR

THE BULLET STRUCK Beatriz's shadow with a flash of purple. The shadow didn't flinch, but every elder in the line stared at the spot where the bullet had struck and watched as the projectile fell to the ground.

Then, they turned their gaze to the woman who fired the first shot.

"She didn't," Beatriz said in front of Jesus, turning around.

"She did," one of Beatriz's comrades yelled.

Before Jesus could grab her, Beatriz ran back to her place in line. After clasping arms, she nodded to the person on her left, then to the one on her right, and together they stormed forward.

By now, Jesus couldn't ignore the pull of the codices. He took hurried steps forward, following the line of elders shielding him. Thin tendrils of purple smoke started emerging from the messenger bag, heading towards the door at the bottom of Chichen Itza.

Veronica fired again, and the rest of Santi's pistoleros joined her.

None of their bullets pierced the elders' shield. The shots fell in the still-growing grass, now above Jesus's knees.

"What are you waiting for?" Hugh screamed to the army officer.

A change came over the man, and he became enraged. At first, Jesus thought it was because a civilian dared question his action. But when the officer turned and commanded his men to take aim, he realized that Hugh's magic had infected the man's mind.

"Shoot them!" the officer yelled, the intensity of his anger matching Hugh's.

More bullets struck the shield of magic created by the elders.

While the bullets couldn't pierce the shield, their momentum had to go somewhere. With just the pistoleros shooting at them, the elders had been able to continue forward. But, with the additional firepower from the troops, they didn't have enough strength; the added force stalled their progress.

Meanwhile, the battle between Balam and Hugh's shadow warrior raged in the dwindling space between the two groups. They rolled and punched, scratched and lunged, neither gaining an advantage.

One of the troops on the right broke away from his group and flanked the elders. Balam, facing that direction because of his ongoing battle, realized Jesus was in trouble and broke away from his fight with the bats, tearing towards the lone troop.

Hugh's shadow took a step forward with its right foot, pursuing Balam, but something held him in place. The grass had closed down around its lower left leg and foot and woven itself together. With a mighty effort, Hugh's shadow pulled its left foot away and placed it in front of the right, half falling and regaining its balance at the last moment. Then, when it tried taking another step, it found its right leg trapped in the same way. Its movement slowed, the shadow warrior turned its expressionless face, along with the black holes where eyes should be, at Jesus.

Jesus stared back and felt like he was looking at a caged beast. He sensed the rage inside the shadow and, by extension, Hugh.

The troop flanking the elders caught sight of Balam before he could pull the trigger. He turned the barrel of his rifle towards Balam and unloaded his clip at the shadow jaguar racing towards him.

The shadow jaguar fell to the ground, sliding forward from his momentum.

"No!" Jesus yelled. There was a part of him that worried about tipping the balance of power in the battle, how Hugh still had his bats and his shadow warrior, where now Jesus just had his shadow warrior. But deeper, and more engrossing, was the sadness from losing a friend, a mentor, and the connection to his ancestors.

Jesus took a step towards Balam. His shadow stopped swatting at the sea of bats for a moment and pushed Jesus's right shoulder, turning his focus back towards the Temple of Kukulcán. Jesus turned back to his shadow warrior, filled with impotent rage, and the warrior clapped the air above them, sending the bats scattering in every direction before looking down at Jesus.

The face was identical to Hugh's shadow warrior—the main difference was in their garb. However, instead of the gaze filling him with anger, Jesus got a sense of cold determination.

He nodded to his shadow warrior and turned back to the main pyramid while his shadow refocused on keeping Hugh's bats at bay.

Ahead of the elders and off to their right, Balam rose to his feet and shook, the vibrations traveling from his head to the tip of his tail. He bounded towards the troop, who was taking aim at the elders again, and launched himself through the air. The collision knocked the troop from his feet, sending his rifle flying through the air.

The troop scrambled away from Balam, towards the weapon, and stopped, still on all fours.

Jesus looked at the rifle. Standing over it, looking down at it, was Abilio.

"I said stay back!" Jesus yelled.

"We both knew that was never going to happen!" Abilio said, picking up the rifle.

He aimed it at the troop, who raised his hands, hurried to his feet, and backed up.

One of the troops still with the main cohort noticed the newcomer to the battle and took aim.

Abilio hurried to the left, heading towards Jesus, and the shots aimed at him hit the elders' shield on the far right.

"I'll make sure nobody comes around," Abilio said, holding the rifle at his side.

Jesus didn't have time for an argument. "Fine. Stay behind me."

Balam looked at Hugh's shadow warrior and discovered the grass slowing his progress. Instead of returning to the battle, he looked at Hugh's bats still swirling around Jesus's shadow warrior's head. The shadow jaguar bared his teeth and rushed forward with a growl.

"My turn," he snarled as he jumped high in the air, clearing Jesus and his shadow warrior, closing his massive jaws around a few of the bats in Hugh's control.

Jesus surveyed the scene. Hugh was yelling and pointing at Jesus and the elders, Santi was nodding behind his pistoleros, and Isabella was staring at the fight in horror with her hands over her ears. The elders were still at a standstill, their purple shields of magic holding up against the incoming bullets but lacking the strength for forward movement.

A tendril of green and brown coming around the side of the pyramid caught Jesus's eye. It snaked down the front of the pyramid, growing thicker as more of it became exposed. Then, more vines appeared, snaking their way towards Hugh and his entourage.

The first vine wrapped itself around Santi's foot and pulled, knocking him down.

"Hugh!" Santi yelled as he turned around, sat up, and dug his free foot into the ground, fighting against the pull.

Hugh took one look at Santi before his bats flew back over the elders and attacked the vines. Their efforts kept those at the center of the attack safe, including Hugh, Santi, Isabella, and the pistoleros, but there weren't enough of the creatures to protect the troops.

The vines grabbed hold of the troop transport vehicles first, pulling them back towards the jungle beyond the Temple of Kukulcán, the vehicles skittering over the ground because of the unmoving tires. Then, as the troops started shooting at the vines instead of the elders, the plants began pulling the troops down and relieving them of their weapons.

Frustrated and furious, the officer in charge of the troops ran towards Jesus, ignoring the wall of elders standing between them. The elders in his way set their feet, bracing themselves so they could absorb the impact on their shield of magic.

The man went right through the shield and barreled into the elders, breaking their chain.

Jesus looked at Abilio in surprise and saw his cousin's eyes were as wide as his.

The pistoleros, unbothered by the vines because of the bats, took aim and fired at the fallen elders. To everyone's surprise, the shield still held, kept alive by the elders' shadow forms.

But now, inspired by their officer, the rest of the troops surged forward, running at the elders.

Jesus's shadow warrior and Balam hurried in front of the elders, knocking as many of the troops away as they could, but some still made it through to the shield. The elders, for their part, never flinched, and accepted the incoming human missiles despite the risk to their own health.

Abilio ran around behind the shield, helping the elders back to their feet and healing them at the same time, his powers benefitting from the four codices present, being on sacred ground, and the proximity in time to the equinox.

Jesus realized that the shield still worked on some of the troops: the tallest, and those with the lightest complexions. The ones who could pass through and barrel into the elders were the ones who looked like they could be his cousins; in short, the ones with Mayan blood. Part of him wished there was some way he could explain to them how helping him would benefit them in the long run, and part of him wished he could ensure they never received the magic returning the codices would give them.

But it wasn't his decision—all of their ancestors had suffered at the hands of the Spanish, and they all deserved their share of their ancestors' legacy.

Jesus looked through the tumult and saw a thin purple rectangle ringed in gold at the base of the Temple of Kukulcán, next to the stone serpent head—space enough for a single person. It cut into the base of the pyramid as if the lowest stone steps weren't even there.

It was time. The spring equinox had arrived.

He looked up at the sun, wondering how his ancestors had ever mapped the stars with any semblance of accuracy, let alone well enough for long-term celestial predictions. Then, he looked at the staircase and the shadow thrown onto it from the pyramid's steps, creating a shadow serpent that ended at the stone serpent head at ground level.

As things stood, he had no way through to the codices' resting place.

Even if the elders somehow surged forward, he knew there was no way they could cross the distance in time.

A sense of defeat coursed through him, punctuated by a profound disappointment that the elders had put their faith in him and he couldn't deliver.

What would happen to these people, these lawbreakers, when the troops took them into custody? What would happen to the codices? And what would Hugh do with everyone around him left defenseless against his power of persuasion?

Jesus wished he could take all of it, all of the upcoming consequences for their actions, their years of feeling like they were less than because of their darker skin and shorter stature, the pain their shared ancestors had felt at the hands of the Spanish.

And in that moment, Jesus realized that he was all of them, every Mayan, and that the door in the Temple of Kukulcán was the beating heart of their culture.

His mother had shown him the truth every year, and every year he ignored her and let her go to the spring equinox at Chichen Itza by herself.

But she wouldn't be alone anymore. None of them would be.

His gift was teleporting objects, bringing them to himself. This time, his self was something more than his physical identity—he was the spirit of every Maya that ever lived, encapsulated in the space behind the shadow door on their most sacred site. He imagined he was inside the room, looking out the door at himself in the distance. Concentrating on the messenger bag with the codices inside, he imagined his shadow grabbing it and placing it in the room, collapsing the physical space between the door and his body.

Except, his own shadow was busy. Hugh had sent his bats against the grass binding his shadow warrior to the ground, and with their help, the shadow warrior was trudging forward as if on a cloud of bats. Jesus's shadow had turned his focus away from the guards and was approaching his counterpart from the side.

But Jesus realized he was greater than a single person, even himself, and his own shadow wasn't required for the task ahead. He continued focusing on the bag he carried as if he had left his body, trusting that a power from the shadow realm would soon emerge and teleport the codices into the room.

The edges of the room started sparking gold, narrowing as the equinox came to an end.

All of a sudden, the shadow serpent that snaked down the stairs of the temple launched forward, the stone head transformed into dark purple magic energy. Weaving through the air like an eel through water, it passed through the back of Hugh's shadow warrior, the force knocking Jesus's shadow warrior out of the way.

Hugh's shadow warrior stood up straight, as if its spine had transformed into a solid piece of metal.

"Kukulcán," the elders whispered, their eyes wide in awe. The troops stared alongside them, everyone motionless.

The feathered serpent god grabbed the codices in its jaws while turning around, then headed straight for Hugh's shadow warrior, who was still between itself and the door.

Hugh let out a scream the second the bag containing the codices touched his shadow. He fell to his knees as his shadow warrior in the field dissolved into nothingness, purple droplets evaporating before they could reach the ground. The bats scattered.

Kukulcán raced back towards the disappearing door. It dove in headfirst, its tail passing the threshold as the door collapsed to a point, then disappeared.

CHAPTER TWENTY-FIVE

In the next instant, the shadow was back on the stairs, inert, off-center by an imperceptible amount because of the traveling sun whose path the ancient Maya somehow calculated centuries before. Everyone stared in stunned silence at the spot on the stairs where the floating feathered serpent had disappeared.

"What the hell was that?" the officer said. He was among the elders, standing still after witnessing the return of Kukulcán. Everyone forgot about the conflict in the presence of a greater power.

Santi shook his head and blinked, as if waking up from a dream. "Were the codices in that bag?" he asked Jesus, more heartbroken than angry.

Jesus nodded. He looked around. Each of the elders, and many of the troops, had faint purple outlines: traces from where their shadow forms merged with their bodies.

The plant growth continued despite the break in the action. The vines and grasses wrapped themselves around the feet of the troops and pistoleros, rooting them to the spot.

Veronica realized first. She started shooting the plants while struggling against her binds.

"Stop," Beatriz said, her voice resonant and powerful.

Veronica looked at Beatriz with her face twisted into a snarl. "Don't you tell me—" she began.

She stopped talking when Beatriz knelt down and put her hand on the ground. The plants started receding.

"I can feel them," she said with a smile. She picked up a seed, holding it in her hand. It grew into a small plant in front of everyone's eyes, then transformed back into a seed before Beatriz turned her hand and let it fall back to the Earth.

"So she does have ripe hands," Jesus said in awe to Balam.

"Ripe hands?" Beatriz asked.

"The plants respond to your call," Balam explained. "Normally, fruit and flowers appear on any plants someone with your power touches, but I'm guessing the extra magic from being here on the equinox boosts what you can do. This power level might not last."

"Even doing this once in my lifetime is enough for me," Beatriz replied, her reverence for the power making her voice catch in her throat.

With the troops no longer preoccupied with the plants attacking them, they all leveled their weapons at Jesus, Abilio, and the elders once more. Some of the ones with Mayan blood, who could feel the magic of their ancestors coursing through their veins, seemed uneasy, and some seemed angry, as if they were proving to their officer that he could still trust them.

Jesus's shadow and Balam came and stood by his side as the groups separated. His shadow warrior laid hands on his shoulders while standing behind him.

"You destroyed public property," the officer announced. "You're coming with us."

"But we aren't the ones who fired the shots!" Jesus said. "All we did was visit the temple."

"You're an international thief." The officer looked towards the group behind him, searching for confirmation. Veronica nodded, Santi looked confused, and Hugh was kneeling, staring at the ground in front of him. Isabella was at the corner of the pyramid, sitting on the ground and leaning on the massive lowest step. The officer waved a finger at Jesus and the elders. "Give yourselves up!"

Jesus called his shadow warrior back into himself; his shadow reappeared, inert, on the ground by his side.

One of the elders, an older woman, stepped forward. Jesus realized it was Gloria, the woman who had lost her husband in the previous weeks. Her all-black garb stood in stark contrast with the colorful dresses the other Mayan women wore.

"Look, I think we need to take a step back and reexamine the situation," she said, her words flowing out of her like honey.

The officer's stern bearing evaporated. He cocked his head and stared at Gloria with softened eyes.

"One young man wanted to visit the temple his ancestors built. His mother and her friends all showed up for the spring equinox. We never fired a shot, nor raised a hand against another person."

The officer shook away his momentary trance and pointed at Hugh. "Then what happened to him?"

"He got in the way of something none of us understand."

Jesus almost interjected with a comment about his tenuous grasp of the phenomenon but kept his mouth shut.

"On the other side, you have a group of guns for hire who put the visitors to Chichen Itza at risk with their bullets. They're the ones carrying guns, and they're the ones you should be taking away in handcuffs."

The officer nodded along with Gloria before fighting back against the spell she cast on him with her words.

"But what about the theft!" he said, pointing at Jesus.

"The codices belong to Mexico," Santi said, his voice heavy. "He stole what was rightfully ours."

Veronica stared at Santi, her eyes filled with hurt.

Santi looked at her with eyes filled with sadness. "I never told you to fire that first shot," he said.

At hearing Santi's words, the officer pointed to his nearest troops and directed them towards the pistoleros. "Take them into custody."

Veronica lowered her weapon, and the rest of her crew followed suit. They let themselves be led to the waiting vehicles, and the troops piled in.

"Let's go," the officer said before climbing back into the passenger seat of the lead car.

Beatriz looked at Gloria when the troops left. "You could have gotten yourself killed!" she said with a mixture of relief and laughter.

"I've always had a knack for talking myself out of situations," she said with a grin.

Abilio took a step towards a nearby elder; they had one knee on the ground and held a swollen ankle.

Jesus put a hand on his cousin's shoulder before he walked away. When Abilio looked at him, he pointed at Hugh.

"Go heal him first," Jesus whispered.

Abilio walked past the elders and Santi before kneeling beside his cousin. He put a hand on Hugh's shoulder, asking how he felt.

Hugh shook his head. "I can't feel anything," he said.

Abilio laid his other hand on Hugh's thigh and closed his eyes. Jesus watched as thin lines of purple magic spread out from his cousin's hands, surrounding Hugh's limbs in a dull purple glow. It continued to the rest of his body, surrounding his torso and working its way up to Hugh's head.

The magic stopped at his eyes, never surrounding him.

Abilio took a big breath and exhaled. His forehead wrinkled with his concentration, and he pushed into Hugh with more force.

"It's no use," Hugh said.

Abilio's magic reabsorbed into his hands. "There's . . . there's nothing else I can do. Maybe if we all put our hands on him? There has to be another healer or two in the group!" he said, looking at the elders.

The elders all looked at Jesus.

Jesus looked at Balam. "Would that work?" he asked.

Balam shook his head no. "His connection to the magic has been severed. You're the only one left who can access their shadow form."

"Wait, what? I thought we gave magic to everyone with Mayan blood!" Jesus said.

"We did, but with it spread among so many, it means that there's not enough for another power like you and Hugh had. Plus, you're twins—that gave you access to more magic than most."

"So other Mayan twins will be more powerful than us?" Beatriz asked, gesturing towards the other elders. She seemed uncertain about speaking with a shadow jaguar.

"For the most part, as long as they're in the Yucatán. I'm not sure how the magic will appear in daily life—there are more Maya today than there were when the priests ruled Chichen Itza, and even then, they never shared the gift."

"It's ok," Hugh said to Abilio, pushing his cousin's hands off of him. He stood up and brushed off his pants. "I'll just have to learn to live without it." He looked at Jesus. "I had no chance against an ancient feathered serpent," he said, trying to lighten the mood.

Jesus smiled. It was the first time they had shared a joke in a long time. "No, I don't think you did."

"But what about the codices? Are they just gone forever?" Santi asked as Abilio healed the elders. With a museum under his guidance, he couldn't help but wonder about the ancient relics. Part of Mexico's heritage, overseas for so long, was back, and now it was buried under tons of limestone.

Jesus approached the pyramid, drawn towards the spot where the codices had disappeared. As he approached, the door reappeared as a dark hole cut into the stone, responding to Jesus's magic. "Come with me," Jesus said to Santi as he passed.

The sun made seeing into the darkened space difficult, but when the two men got close, they could see inside. The four codices were folded and resting on four daises, each of them emitting a soft purple glow.

"They're here, safe, forever," Jesus said. "Home in Mexico—"

"Where they belong," Santi said, finishing his sentence. Santi turned towards Jesus. "You actually did it," the patrón said, as if seeing the codices was more awe-inspiring than the magical display that had occurred mere minutes before.

"You didn't make it easy," Jesus said, remembering the patrón showing up at the museum in Mexico City.

"Your brother can be—could be—very persuasive."

Santi stepped forward, walking into the darkened room . . . out of nowhere, he stopped then pulled back, clutching his face.

"Can't go in unless you have Mayan blood," Balam said from behind Jesus. "And, even then, the room only appears on the equinox unless you're here," he added, referring to Jesus.

"How can people study the codices?" Isabella said.

Jesus looked at Balam. Isabella repeated the question.

"He can take them out if he wants, now that he's the guardian of the Mayan magic," Balam said.

Jesus felt a surge of uneasiness wash over him as he heard Balam's gifted title. He'd never asked for the added responsibility, and he wasn't sure he was ready.

Balam pushed his snout against Jesus's thigh. "Don't worry, you'll know what to do when the time comes."

"Can we see the codices too?" Gloria asked Beatriz.

Beatriz looked at her son with pride. "Ask the guardian," she said.

Gloria and the rest of the elders all looked at Jesus.

Jesus chuckled. "Line up!" he said.

Once the elders were waiting outside the shadow door, he explained that they couldn't, under any circumstances, touch the codices, although he wasn't sure they even could with the magic protecting the documents. He looked at Hugh, who was standing off to the side, dejected.

"You have experience with ancient documents—can you stand just inside the door and make sure only one person goes in at a time?"

Hugh picked his eyes up from the ground. "I'm not sure I even deserve to go in there. Or if I can . . . I lost my magic, remember?"

Jesus waved Hugh forward. "Come on. You still have Mayan blood."

Hugh stood by Jesus's side, and Jesus slipped an arm over his twin's shoulder. "We'll go in together."

They passed through the threshold as one. As soon as they entered, Hugh opened his eyes and relaxed his face when his fear of running into a wall never materialized. He looked back out the door at Santi, still outside.

Hugh inspected the codices, compiled together in one place for the first time in over eight hundred years. He turned around with a smile and poked his head out of the shadow door.

"All right, who's first?" Hugh said, beaming.

Jesus left the room and walked past the elders waiting their turn to see a part of their history. He heard Balam explaining the story of the twelve priests at Chichen Itza to Santi, some of the elders in line listening to every word and others still in awe that a talking shadow jaguar stood right in front of them. Jesus found Isabella standing at the corner of the pyramid, alone.

"You don't want to see the codices?" Jesus asked as he approached.

"I'll see them before I leave," she said, looking off into the distance.

They sat in silence for a while, staring at the manicured lawns around the Temple of Kukulcán that Beatriz had returned to normal.

Both Jesus and Isabella started talking at the same time.

"I owe you an apology," Jesus said.

"I'm sorry I told Santi," said Isabella.

Jesus took the lead in the conversation. "You don't have to apologize—you were just doing your job."

Isabella opened her mouth, but Jesus kept talking.

"I'm sorry for everything. I stole your credit card and spent hundreds of dollars, cost you a trip to Paris, and ruined your time in Madrid on a fake hunt for the thief."

He looked at Isabella as she took a deep, cleansing breath.

"I'm a terrible employee, and an awful friend. And I'm sorry for everything I did to you."

Jesus hung his head. He waited for a moment, and when Isabella didn't say anything, he stood up.

Isabella pulled him back down.

"I understand why you did what you did, and I forgive you." She picked up a small piece of rock from the ground and squeezed. Then, she opened her hand and turned it over, sprinkling rock dust on the ground.

CHAPTER TWENTY-SIX

"And how's the new office working out for you?" Santi said. With one knee on the ground, he reached forward, and Balam walked beneath his outstretched hand. The three of them were near the top of the escalator, in the sunlight pouring in from the museum's large windows.

"Good. There are more people coming by every day," Jesus replied. He suppressed a laugh while watching Santi struggle back to standing in his tight designer jeans.

In the days after the equinox, people had started visiting Jesus and asking him about the odd occurrences in their lives. All of them had Mayan blood, and word had spread in the community that there was someone at the museum who could help them understand what was happening.

Santi, realizing that helping Jesus meet with the visitors could bring more people to the museum, set Jesus up with his own office. He imagined the museum would become a mecca for Mayan people from around the world and had even provided reimbursements for the entrance fee for everyone who met with his new star employee.

Balam stayed with Jesus every day, disguised as a house cat.

Whenever people came by that asked questions Jesus didn't know the answer to, he would lean down, and Balam would whisper the answer in his ear. Few people knew Jesus's real power was object teleportation; most believed he could communicate with animals.

"Do you need a secretary, someone who can handle appointments for you?" Santi asked as they walked together towards the entrance.

Jesus laughed. "Nobody makes appointments; they just show up. Sometimes, they'll come a few days in a row before they get the courage to talk with me."

"And you recognize their face?"

"That, and I can tell they have magic; they always look nervous."

"You can tell?"

Jesus chuckled and said it was obvious.

Santi shook his head. "I'll never understand it," he said. Then, after a few more steps, he said he was going to see Isabella and turned away.

Isabella, after realizing she had received increased strength from the events during the equinox, signed up for a local gym—the first time she had ever lifted weights. There was a bit of confusion about why she got a healthy dose of magic, since she was mestizo—of mixed descent—but it was decided that she must have more Mayan blood than she realized; she was still in the process of investigating her genealogy.

At the gym, she was a new sensation. She didn't look strong at first glance, but she already lifted as much weight as some of the women who had been lifting for years. Jesus was glad his boss was happy and excited about her new hobby, since he still had a bit of guilt left over from his actions while collecting the codices.

Jesus continued on to the museum entrance alone. He watched the visitors streaming in, looking for purple outlines. As far as he knew, he was the one person who could see the magic in everyday life. Together with Beatriz, they decided it was because his magic was still as strong as it had ever been, while hers decreased after the equinox. She could still influence plant growth, but it took hours; it wasn't instantaneous, like it had been at Chichen Itza.

About half of the people coming into the museum had magic. Unsurprising, since there were many people of Mayan descent in Merida. Most went about their trip like it was just another visit to the museum, and Jesus assumed they hadn't stumbled upon their true power, or they had and didn't care about asking anyone's advice. One visitor that day, a sullen-looking teenage boy, looked alone and uncertain, his purple outline from where his shadow merged with his physical form shining bright. Jesus made sure he stood in the boy's path, but the visitor kept his head down as he passed.

Jesus guessed he would see the boy later, or again the following day.

He continued watching the incoming crowd, making himself available for anyone who needed advice about their new gift. His friend Rodrigo appeared at the back of the line, waving at him. His shadow form ringed his body in a purple hue, but he hadn't mentioned anything to Jesus yet.

"Busy today?" Rodrigo said to Jesus when he got in.

"Not as busy as I thought I'd be," Jesus replied.

Rodrigo surveyed the visitors. "See anyone worth approaching?" he said.

Jesus looked at the crowd, searching for Americans Rodrigo could guide instead of signs of magic. He spotted a pair in the back; they looked like they could be Mexican, but he could tell by their clothes that they weren't from there.

"Oh yeah, those could be good," Rodrigo said with a nod when they were pointed out to him.

The pair shifted, and Jesus saw a purple shadow figure the same height as them standing in front of a young woman. But there wasn't a physical body that corresponded to the shadow. When the American pair stepped forward and turned, following the line, Jesus saw a small Mayan girl, not even school-age, walking in front of her mother with a Rubik's cube in hand.

The outsized shadow belonged to her.

Rodrigo followed Jesus's gaze. "What?"

Jesus realized his mouth was hanging open and shut it. "Nothing. Nothing," he said. Seeing a child with such a powerful shadow gave him hope for what Mayan children could do, would do, in the future.

"Here, while I wait for the Americans to get here," Rodrigo said, pulling out his phone. "You heard about the thief in Europe who stole the Mayan writing?"

"Of course, museums everywhere have been talking about it."

"Well, check this out."

Rodrigo stood next to Jesus and showed him a video on YouTube. It opened with a young man at a news desk, talking about the thefts. According to him, there had been a Mexican overseas at the same time as all three thefts, one with ties to a museum in Mexico City.

Jesus's breath caught in his throat. He doubted anyone suspected him, but the mention of a museum made him think that Hugh was a suspect.

Instead, a telenovela star appeared on the screen. The leading man had been on a European vacation between seasons, and there was footage of him attending a red-carpet affair at the Frida Kahlo Museum in Mexico City.

Rodrigo studied Jesus's expression. "What do you think? It has to be him, right?"

Jesus shook his head and laughed. "Maybe," he said. "But I think a handsome guy like him might attract a lot of attention."

Rodrigo pocketed his phone. "There are a ton of theories out there, but this one seems the most likely, to me at least." He looked at the Americans, who were almost through the entrance.

"Also, something weird happened to me at the cenote, man."

Jesus perked up. This was how a lot of his conversations about magic began.

"I dove underwater and kept swimming, no problem. I just came up for air because I knew everyone would worry about me." He lowered his voice to a whisper. "My mom said to come talk to you."

"You have a gift—" Jesus began. His standard first line.

"Hold that thought," Rodrigo said with a smile. He gestured with his chin to the Americans, now walking unaccompanied into the museum. "Time to make some money!" he said, raising his eyebrows in quick succession.

Jesus watched him hurry away. The young mother and the girl with the extraordinary shadow passed by, and Jesus wondered what form her magic would take.

"Excuse me," a deep, timid voice said from his right shoulder.

Jesus turned and saw the sullen teenager standing next to him, his face contorted with nervous anxiety.

"I . . . I was wondering if we could talk."

"Of course, of course," Jesus said, putting an arm on the boy's shoulder and leading him into the museum and towards his office. "What's going on?"

"I hear . . ." The boy looked around and lowered his voice. "Everything."

COULD YOU DO ME A FAVOR?

Please help other readers learn more about this book by leaving a rating and review!

Then head over to my website authormarcoshernandez.com and subscribe to my email list. You'll hear about upcoming releases and deals you don't want to miss!

ALSO BY MARCOS ANTONIO HERNANDEZ

ABOUT THE AUTHOR

Marcos Antonio Hernandez writes from the suburbs of Washington, D.C. An avid reader of both fiction and non-fiction, his favorite authors are Haruki Murakami and Philip K. Dick — in that order.

Marcos graduated from the University of Maryland, College Park with a degree in chemical engineering and a minor in physics. Since graduating, he has worked as a barista, a food scientist, and a CrossFit coach.

authormarcoshernandez.com